To Paulette

A Pie

Thank y … y
me on your show.

Katy xx.

Katy Booth

First Published in 2021 by Blossom Spring Publishing
A Piece of the Jigsaw © 2021 Katy Booth
ISBN 978-1-7398866-2-2
E: admin@blossomspringpublishing.com
W: www.blossomspringpublishing.com
Published in the United Kingdom.

Acknowledgements

A few remarkably talented people have offered encouragement, support and practical help as I wrote this book. I thank Jayne Blunt, Deborah Langley and Gillian Gennard, my incredible beta readers, for their multiple suggestions and improvements. Many thanks to Isobel Vizard, for her amazing ideas and artist's impressions of the Dragon and Porthenby. I also wish to thank Janet and Alan West for their judicious advice, which enabled me to see the wood for the trees and for answering my many questions, whatever time of the day or night. I would also like to include a note of thanks to Steven Longden for the endless cups of coffee and making me laugh every day.

"I get by with a little help from my friends." — The Beatles

For Phoebe, Jasper and Jayne

One Week Before

In the predawn light he played dead. It was the only way out of the nightmare; maybe — just maybe — it would work. He had suffered hours of torment and torture but still had the will to live.

She looked at him with contempt. The game was at an end, she would finish it. This was her favourite part: it made her feel alive. No amount of domesticity could erase this instinct. She flexed her claws and circled the mouse; she could almost feel the crunch of his skull splintering in her mouth.

Strangely, without warning, the cat walked away, leaving the mouse alive. He scampered, as fast as lightning, into the safety of the small crevices that presented themselves in the cowshed.

As the midday sun shone through the slatted walls of the shed, it directed its beams onto the confusion of a web. She had spent hours and hours spinning. Frustrated and exhausted she was unable to get the pattern right; it didn't work. The spider rested a while to survey her work. It was a mess. She resigned herself to the fact she would have to try again…

By early twilight, two swallows were going through their airborne dance in the secluded field that surrounded the shed. Twisting and turning in a well-rehearsed show, they chased their insect prey on the wing but never caught it. Today, their dance was wrong.

Tired and hungry, they perched on the roof of the

shed, watching the insects flit through the air undisturbed. They needed to remember their dance, the routine, the tempo. After conferring, the pair soared into the air, determined this time to give a perfect performance.

He had seen enough; the balance was disturbed. The piskie had felt it in his old bones only a few days ago, and now he had witnessed it for himself. He made his way back to the tribe to report his findings to the elders, wondering how long it would be before the humans decided to take action. Sighing, he hoped against all hope that they would leave well alone. Let the Dragon deal with it. Maybe she could rectify the problem before the humans noticed. If humans interfered, the problem would merely be compounded.

He stood a while and looked out towards the sea. Hundreds of miles beyond the horizon, the storm clouds were gathering, way out to sea where it was rumoured the Dragons convened. He sniffed the air and nodded wisely.

The storm would hit the coast in a week's time.

A Week Later — A Place Called Home

"She was as swift as an arrow. As bright as a rainbow. She took my breath away, such beauty, strength and grace. She was there for a few seconds, and then I wasn't sure I'd seen her at all; maybe it was the early morning sun playing tricks on the restless Cornish sea, building images and wiping them away moments later."

Sam Pascoe's deep, melodious voice filled every corner, nook and cranny of the room. He paused to add dramatic effect, using the moment to check on his daughters' interest. They were captivated by his tale, so he continued.

"I felt overwhelmed. Seeing the Dragon had fired my imagination. When I turned to look at your mother, she was smiling at me, her beautiful grey eyes shining. She knew that I had seen her. That was why she had joined our adventure onto Porthenby Island: she'd suspected the Dragon would be there. And I had been hoping it was because she wanted to meet me!

"Glancing around at the friends who were with us that day, I noticed none of them had seen the Dragon. I had to take long, deep breaths to try to calm my racing heart and stop my hands from shaking. My body was in shock. Your mum's eyes locked onto mine, we didn't say a word. It was our secret.

"Even though your mum lived in Porthenby, that was the first time I'd managed to be in the same group as her. I'd seen her playing volleyball on the beach with a few of her friends but never had the courage to approach her: she was a stunner, out of my league. Edith Treen — her name had a richness to it that drew me in. I imagined she was part of the in-crowd; she was arty and went to the local grammar school, so I didn't think she would have anything to do with me.

"I was thinking too much, that was my problem. She laughed when I told her how anxious I had been when I first met her, saying she'd always wondered why I didn't join in the volleyball games or speak to her.

"The first time I saw the Dragon, over twenty years ago, your mum was waiting to enrol at the art college in Exeter the following September. Over the summer, with the beauty of the Cornish coastline all around us, your mum and I fell head over heels in love with each other."

"Dad, you're such an old romantic." Tamara may have groaned, but Sam knew full well she was secretly enjoying the romance woven through the Dragon story.

Chesten remained quiet. It was the perfect setting for falling in love.

"We spent most of the summer together. She lived with her mother and grandmother across the bay from our farm. By the time September arrived, and your mum went to college, it was obvious we would spend our lives together. The three of us: me, your mum and the Dragon.

"We visited Porthenby Island quite a lot during the long, hot summer, and most times we caught sight of the Dragon. She was magnificent: streamlined, swift and sensational. Every time I saw her, I was enthralled. I'm sure she was aware of our presence.

"We felt very special, being able to see her; not many people could. Maybe the Dragon had chosen us — it felt that way. We understood the need to keep her existence a secret if we wanted her to remain safe and play her vital role in maintaining the balance of nature. For this, she had to live her life in peace and seclusion. If her existence became common knowledge she would be hounded as a curiosity and driven away from the cave. And where would we be then?

"One afternoon while we were picnicking on the island, Edith told me more about the Dragon. On the flood tide she would enter the hazardous strait, which separates Porthenby Island from the headland, swim under the wooden bridge and turn into Mermaid Cave. Once inside she is safe because the cave is always surrounded by the sea, with jagged rocks lining the entrance, making it way too dangerous for us humans to enter. There she rests, on a high ledge where the sea rarely reaches. Her magical breath spurts out of the blowing hole and into the air, cleansing and scouring the surrounding land and sea, helping to remove any impurities. She forms one part of the elements that when combined, constitute an entire ecosystem.

"On the ebb tide, the Dragon swims out of the cave and returns to the open sea. No one knows where she goes. Some people say she meets up with other Dragons and spends her time with them. It is pure speculation though; no one has ever had a sighting of her in the ocean, but she always returns to the Mermaid Cave on the next flood tide.

"Although it's a hard story to believe, I know it to be true. I've seen the Dragon with my own eyes. Even before that day part of me already knew of her existence, just as I knew day followed night. Being as Cornish as a pasty," Sam laughed, "and surrounded by the sea, which is open to the elements, we are very much in tune with nature and understand there are forces out of our control that rule the earth."

As Sam's stories unfolded, they built up a picture of how to live life and how to maintain the status quo, in harmony with nature. The Porthenby Dragon blowing hole story was the girls' favourite. They often joined in the tales they knew by heart. Repeating the words like a well-loved fairy story to be passed on to the next generation, the girls soaked up the folklores of Cornwall. Every time they heard the story, though, something new would strike them, and this time was no different.

"How can the Dragon rest in the cave if it's a blowing hole?" Tamara demanded. "Caves fill up with seawater and the pressure forces the sea upwards, through the blowing hole, into the air. We've studied this at school."

"Not all blowing holes work the same way," Sam said patiently, knowing from past experience that Tamara always needed proof of anything she was unsure of. Doubting Thomas, her mother called her.

"How do you know?" There was a hint of derision in Tamara's voice, which Sam chose to ignore. Although at times her manner could be abrasive, he admired Tamara's questioning attitude.

"Your grandad told me. He's been there with your nan. It's a triumvirate of sea power, wind strength and Dragon might. When the sea powers her way into the cave, the strength of the wind forces it into the portal. Then the Dragon adds her magic breath, which provides an extra boost, rather like a car turbo, and hey presto! The result is the spectacular performance of the marine geyser. She's a piece of the jigsaw, girls. Every piece is needed to make it work."

Sam laughed. He had the knack of making the unbelievable sound quite feasible.

Rumour had it that Sam drew on collective memory stretching back over a long period of time; his stories would bring the past alive with reality and credibility. Anything was believable in this ancient part of the world.

The long, dark winter months and seclusion of Porthenby had encouraged story telling through the ages as a way of passing on information and a source of entertainment. The one and only pub in the cove, The Mermaid's Retreat, was a sounding ground for these stories, and a few people had developed the skill of becoming great narrators: Sam Pascoe being renowned as one of them.

Gathered around a roaring open fire while the weather did her utmost to prevent anyone from venturing outside, stories would gain momentum as they were passed from person to person, group to group and family to family — gaining colour and detail with each retelling. The shared pool of memories helped to build and form the identity of Porthenby. The Mermaid's Retreat was a comfortable, safe place where people were able to express thoughts and ideas in the wrappings of a story. These feelings weren't open to contradiction or ridicule — if they were wrapped in a story.

"How has she managed to remain a secret?" queried Tamara. "Also why haven't I seen her if she exists?"

Chesten sighed and patiently addressed her sister, "If you tell an unbelievable truth and embed it in a story, people tend to think it's not real. Only a few select people have the imagination to know it to be true."

"That's right Chesten," replied Sam reaching down to place another ash log onto the fire. "It's how her existence has managed to remain a secret, known exclusively by a few privileged people. We are the Dragon's guardians. Folk are never certain if the Dragon is a myth or an actuality; it's interesting to juxtapose reality with folklore, people decide which line they choose to believe.

"As for seeing the Dragon, I'm sure one day you will: when the time is right, when you are ready to see her, when or if she needs you…" Sam paused and smiled his wide toothed smile, revealing his front chipped tooth. He broke the ambience by slapping his hands onto his knees and standing up. His daughters knew this to be a sign that story telling was over and jobs needed to be done. The cows would need feeding and checking over.

Chesten glanced over to the window hoping to see some blue emerging from the grey overcast sky. She was disappointed. Relentlessly the persistent Cornish rain continued to torment the rickety windows, it couldn't gain entry even though it would try its hardest to succeed. The storm had hit the coast unexpectedly but was now in her dying throes and beginning to roll away. There had been no weather warnings, no local predictions, no cows seeking shelter or birds hiding under shrubs and bushes. It was a complete surprise, rolling in on the Atlantic Ocean, howling with anger. It had bound the two sisters indoors for a full day, and they were eager to break free of their confinement. Angrily, the rain changed tactics and wheedled the old window frames, rattling the panes of glass, searching for a weak point of entry. It was a failed attempt.

Their home, Cove Cottage, stood defiant against the weather. It had fought against the Cornish rain, stormy westerlies and passage of time for nearly three hundred years and still had a warm welcome for the family, friends and neighbours of the Pascoe family. Nestled and protected in a sheltered cove, surrounded by granite rocks, the cottage harboured its present occupants, the Pascoes, quite happily.

The family could be traced back to living in Porthenby for many years. Some local folk said the family had always been there. Others added that maybe the Dragon also went back to the beginning of time, as we understand it, along with the forces of nature that influence all of our lives by helping to maintain the balance of nature. The steady peaceful running of all the flora and fauna depended on this equilibrium, and the Dragon played her part in this ever-changing jigsaw. Adapting to climate change, the shifting of continents and more recently the impact of human intervention, she was a constant in an ever-changing world.

At that moment Mrs Edith Pascoe burst through the kitchen door with an armful of logs, startling both Chesten and Tamara. They were supposed to be studying for their Easter exams but were both daydreaming about the Dragon story and wondering about the truth of the matter.

The storm had unnerved her. She was conditioned to the changeable Cornish weather and enjoyed the full spectrum of elements that were thrown at the Cornish coast. However, this was different. The ferocity with which the storm had attacked the coast and the short duration it had lasted was peculiar. There was always a build-up to a storm, some kind of warning, but not this time. Cornish storms tended to linger, playing havoc for a few days before they depleted themselves or chose to find another playground to wreak their mischief. This had been a short sharp statement; *nothing good would come of it*, thought Edith. She was apprehensive about what was about to follow but kept this worry to herself.

Edith had heard the ending of her husband's story and laughingly added, "It's like the Cornish piskies, they're also very elusive creatures, nevertheless I'm sure they exist! My workshop keys have been missing, and I've searched everywhere for them. Guess where they were? In my overall pocket. The piskies must have played a trick on me and put them there. I'd already checked my pockets so it's the only explanation!"

Both girls laughed at their mother's joking interruption.

"Unfortunately, the glazing on my recent batch of pottery, which was fired yesterday, hasn't worked properly. I need to start again. It's the second batch ruined this week. I must be doing something wrong. Or it might be the pesky piskies up to their old tricks!"

Mentally checking the recipe for her cobalt blue glaze, Edith wondered if she had changed or omitted anything. Being a very careful and meticulous person, she didn't often make mistakes — especially when it came to her ceramics. The blue was her signature colour, no one else had mastered her technique, and she kept the recipe a closely guarded secret. It had taken her years to perfect but had been well worth the many trials and errors she had endured. With her vivid blue glaze, she had achieved local fame, and her products had leapt in their sales and desirability, turning her solitary cottage industry into an expanding viable business.

Edith preferred to work alone, finding peace and tranquillity in the mixing of colours and the shaping of the clay. There was something very satisfying and positively primeval about taking the clay from the earth, which had formed over a vast span of time, and forging it into useful bowls and jugs. The past working alongside the present in a practical, serviceable way. The process calmed her mind, which enabled her to experiment with making new glazes and developing her style. However, after being encouraged by Sam and the local art college, she was persuaded to pass on her skills and knowledge of ceramics to the next generation of potters.

Edith chose her students carefully and began to employ a few eager up-and-coming potters from around the South West. She had to admit their young enthusiasm was refreshing and inspiring. The students were passionate about their work, and Edith was always there to offer help and support. She knew instinctively when to intervene and when to leave well alone. Allowing young, new ideas to develop with her ceramicists was part of Edith's mentoring philosophy, which her apprentices appreciated. Sometimes, she simply needed to listen to her students as they voiced their problems with their work. Having talked through their difficulty, they would often work out the solution themselves; this enabled them to maintain their individuality and not compromise their own ideas.

"Come on girls," she added softly, banking up the fire with a few more logs. "You've been studying and listening to stories all morning. The weather is changing — looks like the storm has passed over. Why don't you meet up with your friends for a couple of hours of fun? You're only young once!"

Tamara was usually focused on her studies and aimed to gain entry to the art college in Bristol. Her long-term aim was to set up an art gallery in St Ives (hopefully), but realistically she may have to contend with Porthenby until she became famous! Although she was the younger by fourteen months, Tamara stood a couple of inches taller than Chesten, which wasn't very tall.

Revising for her GCSEs was a chore for Chesten, and she longed to be outdoors, whatever the weather. She would often help her father with their herd of South Devon cows, turning them out into the fields for grazing, checking them over to make sure they were healthy and helping with calving. Working alongside her father they had devised a new diet and feeding routine for the herd, which had proved successful, the results being strong, healthy calves. Chesten had become so adept at helping

Sam that he often wondered how he would manage without her.

Despite their differences, or maybe because of them, both girls were close friends and spent many hours talking about art colleges, farming methods, art studios, prize bulls and of course boys.

"Fancy going to Porthenby Beach, Ches?" asked her sister. "There's bound to be a few of our friends meeting up there."

"Yeah, I need a break," yawned Chesten as she untied her long, wild red hair from its scrunchy. The log fire, studying all morning and listening to their father's Dragon tales had made her a little languid. She needed to get outside and allow the fresh air to liven her up. Tamara would often say jokingly that Chesten's hair was the same coppery red as their cows. Chesten thought the cows were a beautiful colour and laughed off the resemblance. Far worse comparisons had been made. Love it or hate it, her hair made a statement. Tamara also knew the untying of her sister's hair meant no more studying; it was a time for playing.

Slamming her history of art book on the kitchen table, Tamara picked up the discarded scrunchy and tortuously drew back her short, dark, bobbed hair into a tight ponytail, much better for beach attire. Both girls darted for the back door and stepped out into the elements. They were pleased to find clear blue skies and a watery sun, which was trying her best to coax the spring flowers into a growth spurt. Such changeable weather was normal for Porthenby and made the girls feel secure and relaxed, the day would be just like any other — which was as it should be.

"Don't forget to check on the blowing hole," Edith shouted from the back door, as the girls waved goodbye to her.

Being a quiet, thoughtful woman Edith was highly respected in the local community and was considered to be a sage. Learning, over time, to keep her opinions to herself and listen to the concerns of others, she was able to offer her valuable advice, when it was sought and not a moment before. With this ability Edith was able to define when things were different, not normal, not right, out of kilter, not as they should be. This was quite a difficult task, as everyday life often includes a few atypical incidents, nonetheless Edith had perfected her skills and was able to identify unusual occurrences, and in doing so had gained the trust of the local community.

Sam, sensing the girls may have picked up on their mother's anxious tone, called them over to the barns to look at a day-old calf, which appeared decidedly healthy, being strong boned and bright eyed. The ancestry of Sam's herd could be traced back to the Norman Invasion, when the cattle had been brought over from Normandy by the invading conquerors. They were fine specimens. "See girls, everything is hunky-dory here. Check on the blowing hole, for your mother, but I'm sure it's working perfectly well and will stay that way. Enjoy yourselves girls, I'll tell you a story about the Dragon when you return."

Strolling down the hill from their farm towards the beach, the girls felt exhilarated as the sea breeze raced against their bodies, welcoming them outdoors. A comfortable silence trickled into the personal space between the two sisters and flowed over the stresses and strains of the day, erasing any anxiety which may have presented itself, like soft rain smoothing out the rough edges of sandstone. As they neared the town, Porthenby appeared to greet them by warming their skin in the gentle spring sun. The girls relaxed and relished their freedom from the confinement the storm had created.

The town was situated on Cornwall's rugged north coast. Accessible by a solitary, winding, single track road, it had escaped the notice of the hordes of tourists who holidayed in Cornwall over the summer months. The locals said the Cornish piskies played their part in this seclusion by mischievously turning around signposts and sending curious, adventurous tourists along a rutted farm track back onto the road that led away from the cove. Muttering under their breath, the visitors would face frustration and confusion at their inability to find their way around the area. Some would leave with punctured tyres and damaged exhausts, which had been knocked off by a few well-placed boulders, another piskie prank. The residents would laugh at the supposed piskies' interference and leave the altered signposts and boulders well alone. For the few persistent visitors who did manage to find Porthenby, they found the lack of touristy facilities disappointing. With very few cafes, ice cream parlours and souvenir shops, not surprisingly the tourists didn't choose to stay for very long, which suited the locals.

Porthenby's seclusion was safeguarded. It was a place where secrets could be kept.

Hidden Monster

As the sisters walked through the cobbled street leading to the beach, they saw Old Ben. He was busy in his garden tending the vegetable plot, his usual morning routine. He was retired now, but was once, many moons ago, the local postman. Having held the position for a number of years and being of a friendly disposition, he was quite knowledgeable about the people and families of Porthenby: who was related to whom, where they originated from, family feuds and arguments; nothing got past Old Ben.

He had never been in a hurry to complete his postal rounds and would happily chat and pass the time of day along with anyone who chose to speak with him, which was most people. They would share snippets of information and gossip; this formed a network of news that spread throughout the community — like wildfire.

"Hello girls, are you going to the beach?" queried Ben, as he leaned on his spade. Retirement had loomed threateningly upon Old Ben. It was like the monster creeping out of the cupboard at night to scare the young Ben, who had been told he would be safe when he was tucked up in his bed. In those childhood days, when his mother had put him to bed, he had begged her to stay with him — just for a while longer. He was certain that the monster wouldn't torment him if his mother was present, then he would be able to sink peacefully into slumber. But she had been adamant that there wasn't any such thing as a monster in the cupboard. Unfortunately, he found out that wasn't true. When the door to his bedroom was shut firmly behind her, the monster would creep out of its hiding place and terrify him. He was a little boy, alone in the dark, sobbing into his pillow, unable to call for his mother; she wouldn't come.

Eventually he outgrew the monster. He learnt not to tell anyone about it, realising people would think he was peculiar. However, when things preyed on his mind or upset him, the monster would stick its foot in the door of the cupboard and snarl at him, threatening to come out. In a menacing voice the monster would growl, "I'm going to get you Ben! Fee! Fie! Foe! Fum! I smell the blood of an old postman."

Anxiety increased as his retirement date approached, and the monster grew in size, ferocity and brutality. Many sleepless nights were endured in an effort to avoid the terror that stalked him in the drifting grey time between wakefulness and sleep. He kept these worries to himself. He envisioned his twilight years filled with a lack of communication and contact with people, loneliness. Surprisingly, after the fateful day had passed by, he adapted to his new situation by spending quite a lot of time in the garden and chatting to the people who were passing by. He found he wasn't lonely at all. In fact, he could spend far more time nattering, now that he wasn't delivering post, which suited him well. His night times were his own again; the monster had disappeared.

Some people called him "Nosey Ben". However, Edith always said he was a valuable source of information, Porthenby needed more people like him. Ben thought she was a kind woman, so understanding and easy to talk to.

"Have you heard about Liz Rowe's hens?" Ben asked. "They haven't laid for two days now, not one of them.

She asked me to pass that snippet on to your mum. Also, Mrs Tallack's dog Rossi, you know the cute little spaniel who wouldn't hurt a fly? Well, he barked at Bill the new postman yesterday and today he tried to bite him. Might be nothing, even so I'm sure your mum should know about it."

"Thanks Ben," acknowledged Chesten. "I'll let mum know as soon as we get back. How are you today?"

"Top of the world, can't complain," replied Ben, theatrically waving his arms around in the air making a world shape with them.

Chesten noticed the concerned look flicker across Ben's face, directly before his smile broke through. He waved to the girls, and turned back to his spadework as they strode towards the beach.

All these strange goings-on in Porthenby were starting to worry him and he didn't need that. He had heard the monster stirring in the cupboard again last night. The menacing voice at first quiet and unsure gained volume and momentum as the darkness of the night became all consuming. Old Ben covered his ears, but could still hear the monster as it started to bellow, "One… two… three… four… five… six, seven, eight, nine, TEN! Coming ready or not!" The old playground chant that incited giggling and frivolity in his school friends, as they raced off to find a hiding place, now caused deep rooted fear when it was repeated by a devilish voice in the middle of the night. It made him shiver and filled him with a sense of dread. He hoped things would settle down soon.

As the girls continued towards the beach, Chesten pondered about what Ben had told them.

Liz Rowe's hens were content, well fed and cared for. She kept a tidy hen coop and her flock was healthy. At this time of the year, with the daylight hours stretching out and the spring sun warming their bodies, the hens should be laying every day. Liz was renowned for her delicious free range-eggs, as she branded them. This made Chesten smile, they were more like wild hens, having the run of the garden and the surrounding fields.

In the late afternoon, Liz would call the hens in for their special treat of the day that she had prepared: rice one day, spaghetti the next, roasted vegetables; whatever leftovers that were available. She would stand at the hen coop and yell at the top of her voice, "Chickens!" As if by magic the hens would appear, greedy for their treat. Tearing across fields, scrambling out of hedge bottoms, flying out of bushes — eager to claim the treats. It was hilarious to watch.

Occasionally, Chesten would take a treat for the hens, always timing her arrival so she could watch them being called in to roost. They reminded her of prehistoric animals tearing across the field, their wings firmly tucked in and displaying a stocky body with a definite dinosaur shape. Having a peculiar way of moving, lurching from side to side, reinforced the image. The hens were good layers and amazingly always deposited their eggs in the nest boxes. Liz said it was because she made the boxes warm and comfortable, so the hens felt secure there; tucked away safely from prying eyes and predators. If the hens weren't laying, then something was wrong.

As for Mrs Tallack's cute little spaniel, Rossi, who wouldn't hurt a fly — that was another kettle of fish. The dog had a mean streak which ran through his body. One day he would be fine, wagging his tail and pleased to see you, the next day he was grumpy and snappy. Mrs Tallack, who adored the dog, had a way of rewriting history. She had told people how sweet natured her dog was so many times, and now she actually believed it. Some of her friends whom the dog had growled at or bitten, were surprised when this happened, as they had also chosen to believe the fabrication of the dog's nature rather than the reality. Rubbing the scar on her finger, where the cute little dog had snapped at her when she had reached out to pat his head, Chesten decided she didn't need to trouble her mother with this story.

A Meeting Place

As the cobbled lane ended, giving way to the beach, a group of local teenagers were taking advantage of the break in the weather to meet up and spend time together. It was the first few days of the Easter holidays, time to enjoy fooling around, catching up with friends and enjoy the beginning of spring — as well as being young. Chesten scanned the group of teenagers, searching for a tall, slim figure with dark curly hair and flecked hazel eyes that reminded her of the autumnal colours in the fields around Porthenby. She was looking for Jack Lee, the personification of Heathcliff, her wild romantic lover (in her wildest dreams). However, she was no Catherine Earnshaw, with her Titian hair and pale freckled skin.

"Who are you looking for?" Tamara demanded.

Jack, who had been casually glancing around the beach for the past hour, hoping Chesten would appear, was waving and striding across the beach towards them.

"Oh, it's him!" Tamara's sharp grey eyes picked out the tall, angular youth from the gang of friends. "Remember to play it cool, don't make it so obvious you like him." There was a touch of resentment in her voice. Jack Lee seemed to be taking over a lot of her sister's attention and time these days. She knew her feelings were unreasonable, but Tamara felt as though the ties with her sister were being loosened, and Jack was the reason why.

"I won't," promised Chesten.

Jack's family had settled in Porthenby before he was born, sometime during the early sixties. They bought a house and decided to set down roots with a view to raising a family in the quiet sleepy cove. When the Lee family arrived, they helped the local farmers — at first by being an extra pair of hands. They tended the flocks of sheep and the herds of cattle and horses, instinctively knowing how to deal with timid sheep, awkward horses and stubborn cows. The animals seemed to trust the Lee family implicitly. It was the same when they worked on the land, they knew when to plant the seed as well as which fields suited which crops. The family was welcomed by the locals and settled into the Cornish cove quickly and easily. They had a magic touch and were born farmers the locals said. According to Jack's grandad, the family had felt Porthenby was the place to settle because there was an air of magic about the place. The family knew they could blend in and make a good life there.

It wasn't long after moving into Porthenby that they had started to build up their own flock of sheep, selecting ewes that exhibited good breeding characteristics to develop their own stock of specialist sheep with exceptional fleeces. With their unequivocal good practice around livestock, their flock had built up over the years and currently consisted of over three hundred breeding ewes. They were in demand amongst wool spinners throughout the country.

Jack, dressed casually in baggy shorts and loose T-shirt, ran over to meet the two girls. Chesten's heart skipped a few beats and she released a deep audible sigh.

"Hi girls, great to see you both," enthused Jack turning his attention directly to Chesten. "My mum would like to come over to your house later today. She's a bit concerned about our sheep — maybe I could come as well?"

"Yes of course, we would love to see you, wouldn't we Tam?" replied Chesten enthusiastically.

Tamara realised her sister had not registered or acknowledged the problem with the sheep, even though their mum had always stressed they were to report anything unusual to her immediately: such as when things were different, not normal, not right, out of kilter, not as they should be. Neither Chesten nor Jack seemed to be taking the occurrence seriously, they were too engrossed with each other. Annoyed, Tamara stepped in, "What's wrong with the sheep, Jack?"

"Oh, the sheep," replied Jack tearing his focus away from Chesten's sea green eyes and facing Tamara. "Well, as you know lambing season is well under way and disappointingly only two hundred and thirty of the flock have lambed. There's a few more to lamb, but there's no way we will reach our expected target of two hundred and ninety, and my dad's usually spot on with his predictions when it comes to lambing time. We always take bets on the number of lambs that are going to be born, and he wins every time. My dad says something's not right, we need to see your mum. Should we come over to yours after dinner tonight?"

"Yes, that's fine," gushed Chesten hardly able to conceal her delight at the thought of seeing Jack later that day. "I'll have a word with mum when we get back. I'm sure she mentioned having a residents' meeting tonight at our house. People are coming over to talk about things not being right. Did she say seven o'clock Tam?"

Tamara muttered her agreement and sulkily glanced over to Porthenby Island. She would have to endure Jack Lee again this evening, and in her own home. Would this never end?

Fantasy Island

Rising dark and sheer from the defensive ocean, the island was an impressive spectacle. Access from the headland was allowed via a rickety wooden bridge, making it both forbidding and enticing depending on how you read the message. The blowing hole was on the sea facing side of the island, welcoming the flood tide and spewing out sea fumes into the Cornish air. It looked fine. Tamara scrutinised it from the beach but felt she needed to get a closer look. It could also be a way of ridding themselves of Jack.

"I'm going over to the blowing hole to check on it," Tamara said peevishly. "Mum reminded us this morning to check and make sure everything was as it should be." Her mother could be very elusive at times, but she did seem anxious this morning and if checking on the blowing hole would alleviate her anxiety then Tamara would do it. "Are you coming, Ches?" Tamara started to stroll over towards Porthenby Island, hoping her sister would follow and leave Jack behind.

"Wait Tam, I'm coming with you!" shouted Chesten, reluctantly turning away from Jack.

"I'm coming too," added Jack, as he determinedly followed both girls towards the island.

Tamara groaned inwardly as Chesten and Jack fell in pace with her. It wasn't as if Jack was an unlikeable person, far from it — he was chatty, sociable and good looking. Of course, it was unreasonable, but she always enjoyed times spent alone with her sister. Having a growing sense that perhaps things were about to change disturbed her. She needed to get a grip on the situation or become the jealous sister.

Jack chatted to both girls as they walked across the grassy headland towards the bridge, which separated the island from the mainland. It was the dividing line between reality and fantasy — according to folklore. A breeze had emerged, which became stronger, whipping up the waves on the flood tide. Enabling the white horses to stampede towards the beach and crash into the rocks and caves.

"The blowing hole will be awesome today," Chesten enthused. "In fact, I'm sure I can hear it!" Turning to her sister she joked, "It's a perfect day for the sea fumes to work their magic." It was an attempt to try and appease Tamara's sulky mood, being aware her sister resented Jack's presence.

Jack looked quizzically at Chesten, "What magic?"

"Look, you can see the spray billowing out!" continued Chesten, ignoring Jack. The spray acted like a prism, diffusing the spring sunlight into a vast rainbow, which spread across the sky above the blowing hole. It was magnificent.

"It looks beautiful," murmured Tamara.

The sheer force of the sea spray exploding out of the blowing hole caused the ground to tremble slightly. It was disconcerting for most people, but Chesten, Tamara and Jack had known this place forever and were happy to be there. The ocean demonstrating its strength animated them. Jack stopped shortly before the bridge and laid his hands flat against the turf; eagerly the girls followed suit. It was a game most of their friends played. On the flood tide the mighty power of the waves, crashing against the rocks as they forced their passage through the entrance of

Mermaid Cave, shook the ground gently. The pressure exerted by the waves was transferred through the rocks, earth and into their bodies.

"Wow," whispered Tamara, turning and smiling at her sister.

Chesten jumped up and sprinted towards the bridge, eager to be the first to reach it. It was always a race between the sisters.

"Hey, cheat! You've got a head start!" Tamara shouted, darting after her, closely followed by Jack.

He had enough sense not to overtake them.

Halfway across the bridge, Chesten stopped to draw breath and enjoy the thrill of the flood tide. Her senses became alive with the sight, feel, taste, sound and smell of the ocean — it never failed to please her. Tamara took her rightful place: beside her sister. She knew how much Chesten loved to be here — on this bridge.

Tamara peered over the hand bar into the waters below when suddenly something caught her eye. It was something in the tumultuous waters swirling around the rocks at the entrance to the strait. The flood tide was making it difficult for her to focus on one point, everything was in constant motion, forever changing. The something was colourful, an array of blues and greens, mixed together, expanding and contracting, never seeming to gain shape. Her peripheral vision seemed to give a better view and suggested a long sleek shape. But as she tried to focus it would break up and disappear in the myriad of blues, which comprised the Cornish sea. She glanced at Chesten, who seemed to be preoccupied with Jack, smiling, and laughing with him. "Ches, look over there," Tamara said, pointing to her sighting. "I'm not sure... I think there's something swimming there, something massive."

Turning away from Jack, Chesten looked to where her sister was pointing and was met with the greys and blues of the swirling energetic sea tearing its way toward them. She studied the area as Tamara urged her to keep looking.

"I can see it!" yelled Jack.

Tamara tried to dismiss Jack's claim and turned her back to him, this wasn't how it should be. He shouldn't even be here with them.

"Look at the colours over there, Ches!" Jack pointed to a swirl of blues, greens and greys, which were quickly converging and separating as though they were playing tag with the ocean.

Chesten searched where Jack was indicating, leaning into him as she peered over the hand bar. "I've got it!" she shouted above the deafening ocean. She screwed her eyes, scrutinising the colours, moments later she was able to make out a faint shape. It was big, probably too wide to make its way through the narrow corridor but also amazingly supple. With a series of practised twists and turns it negotiated the entrance to the strait easily and confidently. The route was familiar.

"What is it?" screeched Tamara, grabbing hold of her sister for confirmation of what they had witnessed. The shape disappeared into the depths of the sea as an enormous wave crashed through the passageway, carrying the vision under the bridge and back out into the ocean. Suddenly Tamara felt excluded. Her sister had turned to Jack, they were smiling at each other, they were sharing the experience together.

"What did we see?" queried Chesten, quickly turning and looking at her sister; aware that she would need her undivided presence and attention.

"I'm not sure we saw anything," replied Tamara sharply, "maybe it was a trick of the light." She wasn't going to admit that maybe, just maybe, they might have seen the Dragon. Not with Jack there, he shouldn't be part of this experience.

Chesten nodded in agreement. Sometimes, usually after their dad had told them a Dragon story, their imaginations were more susceptible to unusual happenings. Inexplicably it had seemed so real, and they had all seen something.

Maybe it was a sea monster, suggested Jack who was beginning to doubt what he so clearly saw moments before.

"Sea monster," guffawed Tamara, trying to dismiss Jack's credibility. "You can't be serious. It's the ocean playing games with us."

Jack was clearly uncomfortable with Tamara's comment, and as Chesten didn't want to embarrass him further she was gentler with her reply saying maybe it was a shoal of fish, they often acted that way. Jack didn't seem totally convinced by this explanation, but hoping to claw back some credibility with Chesten, he nodded in reply.

The sighting had rekindled a memory in Jack, he thought back to when he had been a young lad, when his father had tucked him up in bed at night. Jack had often pleaded for a story, but his father was no storyteller and would encourage Jack to choose his own book and read it himself. He had always singled out books about sea monsters, his favourites. His father told him that when he had been a young boy; he had made a connection with a sea monster, a massive force whose presence he'd sensed through the wall of an under the sea tin mine, a submarine mine. Jack had been fascinated and begged his father for more information. Nothing more to tell, his father had said, adding he'd suspected it was the Dragon and from that day on he knew that she truly existed. It was their secret, his father had said. He shouldn't have been in the tin mine and nothing good would come of it if they told other people. Jack kept the secret and today he had witnessed the sea monster for himself. He was sure of it.

The moment passed and reality filtered back into their young lives. As both girls stepped off the bridge and onto the island, the tension was broken.

"Fantasy Island," the sisters chorused. Most of the local kids spent hours playing there or meeting up with friends, but for Chesten and Tamara it was a second home, full of childhood adventures and memories. Together with their dad's stories about the magical qualities surrounding the island, the realities and myths had become ingrained and were part of them.

Jack smiled at the girls, pleased to be part of the adventure, "You're both crazy!" he shouted over the blustery wind.

Chesten knew it wasn't fish they had seen, the outline of the object was blurred, but it had kept its shape for longer than a shoal of fish would, particularly in such turbulent water. If it wasn't fish, what could it be? Was it the Dragon? Was she a real entity? Part of her always considered her dad's stories to be fantasy with perhaps a little bit of truth sprinkled through, but this…? She would have to talk to her mother when she returned home. Edith would know what to make of it.

A Strange Find

Isolated and imposing, Porthenby Island towered above the beach, looking directly west over the vast Atlantic Ocean. No land mass stood between the island and the coast of America, over three thousand miles away. Who knew what life forms hid in those murky depths? Most people imagined they knew what lay beneath the sea, but there was a lot of uncharted territory holding secrets yet to be discovered.

The island could be walked around in twenty minutes and consisted of springy turf, caused by generations of rabbits digging and making their burrows. Undulating ground provided hiding places for children to play games of hide and seek, and also for hares to scrape out their forms. The remote location provided sanctuary for many different species of animal that wouldn't fare so well on the mainland, where natural predators such as foxes and dogs were abundant. It was their haven.

Evidence found around the island confirmed there had been settlements on the site reaching back to the Stone Age. So many people and creatures had lived and died there, eons before the present day, and Sam Pascoe believed their collective memories were held and cradled in the ground. He wove many of his stories around the Dragon living alongside the numerous people who had made a life on the island. According to Sam, they had lived in harmony with nature, both the Dragon and the people, hand in hand.

Reaching the sea facing cliffs was intoxicating as the wind and sea spray danced around in the salty air, causing Chesten's hair to tangle and snarl, animating it. Tamara imagined that it resembled Medusa's snakes, but her sister was no monster. Being unable to imagine any monstrous situation her sister would lead her into that would cause distress or danger, she quickly shook the dark clouds from her head.

Bursting into the air, with a myriad of sea colours, the mist from the blowing hole was brighter, more dazzling than the usual grey green mist, which normally presented itself.

"So bright," enthused Chesten.

"Cool," added Tamara.

"There's something on the grass over there," indicated Jack as he walked over to the object.

Tamara was annoyed with Jack who, she assumed, was trying to take the lead. She glanced over to where her sister and Jack were walking. Reluctantly she followed them.

At the cliff edge they noticed swirls of foamy water, tinged with silver, that spread over a large oval shape. The shape was bright and luminous with a rainbow of colours swimming across its surface, like oil spilt on water. Jack bent down to pick it up and Chesten leaned in to get a closer look. She carefully took the object out of Jack's hands and turned it over, feeling the flat surface and edges glide along her fingers. "So smooth, you can hardly feel it," she mused. Bending the object, she found it extremely pliable. Thinking back, to the well-rehearsed performance of the image moving through the strait, it occurred to her that it could be a scale. Before she could voice her ideas Tamara jumped in.

"It looks like a scale!" declared Tamara. "Could it be from the creature?" She didn't seem the least bit concerned about openly ridiculing and dismissing Jack's sea monster theory, merely a few minutes ago. Finding the object and being able to hold it, seemed to reaffirm to the group that they had witnessed something, and the something was a creature.

"It's huge," added Jack. "What kind of animal would have scales like this?"

"Something massive. Maybe prehistoric?" Chesten suggested.

"Oh, Ches, your imagination runs wild at times," laughed Tamara.

In that moment, Jack realised Chesten knew of the Dragon's existence. He loved the idea that she assumed it could be a creature from prehistoric times. He'd thought the same but being determined to present himself as a cool character in her company, was hesitant to voice his ideas. He wouldn't present himself for ridicule again. "Let's take it home and google it. There isn't any internet here," Jack said, taking hold of the object and examining it himself.

"Sounds like a good idea to me," replied Tamara, snatching the object out of his hand.

Tamara found it difficult to dislike Jack, even though she tried her hardest. He was annoyingly attentive to her ideas, never dismissive of her and always made her feel welcome in his company. She tried not to feel resentful towards him. He must have noticed her offhand manner, and yet he still spoke gently and kindly to her. She wished she didn't feel this way — he wasn't that bad.

The threesome walked home excitedly, chatting about what they had seen and found. A friendship group was beginning to form, which allowed speculation of ideas to be expressed safely. With his relaxed, carefree ways and ability to make people feel special, Jack was beginning to wheedle his way into the sisters' company. Chesten was pleased that Jack was making such an effort with Tamara. Her sister could be very awkward at times, especially if she felt excluded from anything that involved Chesten. Looking at Jack chatting to Tamara reinforced her opinion of him, he was a special person. The Lee family definitely had a magical touch.

It wasn't until they were back on the beach that Tamara realised she had enjoyed the walk back from the island, even though Jack had been with them; or maybe it was because he had been there. Perhaps he wasn't so bad after all…and Chesten and Jack did look good together. Her artist's eye could appreciate that. Somehow, they seemed to gel.

Tea Time

"Lay the table girls, tea is nearly ready," Edith called to her daughters who were upstairs choosing their outfits for the evening's meeting. She had been in a reflective mood all afternoon, after listening to the account of their visit to Porthenby Island and the sighting. Motor memory took over as she prepared a selection of sandwiches while Sam diced slices of carrots and celery to accompany their tea. He knew to remain quiet while his wife was thinking things through. She didn't need fragmentation of her thought process at a time like this. Presenting the scale to Edith had added to her state of concern, which had started to form a couple of days ago with the unusual happenings around Porthenby. Together with her daughters' description of the colours streaming from the blowing hole and the sighting of the creature, Edith knew she needed to take action… but what type of action? The girls had been overwrought when they returned home. It had been difficult to follow any line of their hasty gabble. Both talking at once, all she could hear was the odd word from each girl… monster, prehistoric creature, massive body, twisting, turning. Edith's head was spinning with the overload of information. She felt rather than heard the anxiety, or was it excitement, in their voices? This was so out of character for her daughters and further added to Edith's worried state of mind.

Sam had told the girls to calm down so they could get some sense out of them. Both girls had looked at each other and started laughing. Ever since they were very young children Chesten usually let Tammy chatter away and then would add her own part. Quite content to listen without interrupting her, she realised, without being told, she was encouraging her shy sister to talk by allowing her the space and time. Of course, that didn't happen all the time — they were sisters after all, but that was the normal run of things, even though Tamara wasn't a shy young girl anymore. And today was presenting itself as anything but normal.

"We've seen the Dragon!" Chesten declared. "She swam through the strait and under the bridge that leads to the island. Jack saw her too."

"We knew it was her. She's massive," added Tamara. "We've been searching online for a match for the scale and haven't found a thing! I can't understand it, there's always some kind of link on the internet."

The girls continued with their account as Edith and Sam listened patiently, encouraging them to remember everything they had seen.

"Well girls, it sounds to me as though you've definitely had a sighting of the Dragon," Sam declared. "You won't find any answers on the internet, the Dragon is too elusive. Also, the piskies play their skilful part extremely well in protecting her seclusion, making it difficult to find her. Anything posted on the web they tamper with and present as a spoof, rather like the Loch Ness Monster stories. And now the Dragon has decided to reveal herself to you. It was simply a matter of time before you saw her, she trusts this family. Young Jack too! Mind, I'm not surprised there — the Lee family have always had a way with animals, the magic touch. I think the three of you need to keep this quiet, we'll keep the talk amongst ourselves. People who don't believe can have sharp tongues and say hurtful things. We know the truth of it, that's enough."

Both girls seemed happy with Sam's reasoning. They were good at keeping secrets.

Edith would need to talk with Phoebe about the Dragon when she arrived for the meeting tonight. Her mum was always willing to offer suggestions and usually the guidance was to leave well alone. The Dragon would sort it out, as she did in the case of the oil disaster. Such devastation to the environment, and yet even when faced with wide-reaching destruction the Dragon had managed to put things right. But at times the Dragon had needed help, and on one such occasion Phoebe Treen, Edith's mother, had tended the Dragon in her hour of need. It had all fallen onto Phoebe's young shoulders: there was no one else who could help. After all, she was basically one of a handful of people who believed in the Dragon… and who had seen her.

"Stop worrying, Edith," Sam murmured quietly, interrupting her thoughts. "You will think of something, your family always does."

Edith noticed Sam was absent-mindedly worrying his chipped tooth, his front incisor, which transformed his smile into a cheeky grin. It was a habit that presented itself when he felt stressed; his quiet voice and demeanour didn't fool her. By family, Sam was referring to her forefathers, who had passed down the Porthenby Dragon stories from parent to child, forming a vast collection over time. So many voices and styles all agreeing on one thing: the importance of the Dragon's wellbeing, which enabled her to continue her magic and help maintain the natural order. Sam had greedily encouraged Edith to share all of her tales with him. He had been the perfect audience, listening intently and asking pertinent questions where relevant. Sam had the knack of storytelling and, over time, Edith's details and past happenings concerning the Dragon began to form the foundations for his own narratives. She was the voice; he was her narrator.

Edith's family always seemed to understand intuitively how to deal with the Dragon. Her mother's recommendation was usually to leave well alone, but Edith wasn't confident in her own judgement and actions and needed to confer with her mother. She wondered what would happen if she was unable to solve this issue, and if action was necessary to protect the survival of the Dragon. The Dragon was losing her scales, which was a very worrying sign. Something had changed drastically to cause this. Edith needed more information, and hopefully the meeting tonight would enlighten her. She needed to rest before the gathering, so that she would be able to listen intently, then she might be able to make sense of what was happening. After all, the oil disaster was an obvious catastrophe, one that stood up and slapped you in the face, but this problem was elusive, hiding behind all the effects and obscuring the cause. Hopefully, tonight would reveal some leads which could be followed up, then she would be able to make her decision.

The Disaster

"Your nan always offered a very factual, balanced account when retelling her stories, probably due to her background in journalism. She listened to people's opinions and first-hand experiences. It's what made her stories so colourful, they had so many voices running through them," Sam said to his daughters, as they were sitting enjoying the warmth of the log fire, waiting for the assembly to start. "She was a very practical person. Still is, capable and confident in her decisions and actions. During the time of the oil disaster, your nan was a junior reporter with the local newspaper and had access to quite a few influential people: local councillors, business people, the mayor, police officers, MoD officials, which proved invaluable when the disaster hit.

When I first met up with your mum she invited me to her house for tea, and the conversation eventually came around to the oil disaster. Phoebe was willing to talk about it, and I was intrigued to find out her opinion and perceptive on the catastrophe. Hearing first-hand accounts of events always offers something new, and I was eager to hear her views. She said it helped to keep memories alive by retelling stories. I learnt a lot from your nan, I still do."

Phoebe entered the room at that moment in her usual brisk manner, introducing the cool evening air into the warm cosy cottage. Although small in stature she was a formidable presence in any setting, oozing confidence and capability.

"Nan," shrieked Tamara, as she ran over to give her grandma a big hug, virtually lifting Phoebe off the floor. "We've seen the Dragon! Today at the island!"

"Steady," soothed Phoebe, as she hugged her granddaughter back. "Well, I'm glad you've seen her. I knew you would at some time. Did you see her as well Chesten?"

"Yes, come and sit over here by the fire, I've saved your favourite chair."

"I'll make some tea," Sam announced, "while you get warmed in front of the fire. I was about to tell the girls about the oil disaster, but now you're here you might like to take over the story. But first you'll need to listen to the girls' report of the Dragon!"

Unfolding the events of the day to their grandmother, Phoebe became an engaged listener as they filled in every detail of their adventure. Asking questions where necessary, to move the story along, she enticed all the relevant information from them. Satisfied the story was complete, she took hold of her granddaughters' hands. The firelight flickered on Phoebe's face, smoothing out the wrinkles and effects of time, creating a younger more vibrant person.

"Listen carefully girls, this is important. You are both young and impressionable, don't let your heart rule your mind. It seems to me the Dragon has chosen to reveal herself to you. I knew she would, at some time. The question is why now? I'm sure that question will be answered in time. Maybe she needs something… or maybe you have been chosen to carry her story on. Don't assume because she's made you aware of her that she needs your help or that something has to be done. At times it's best to leave well alone. The Dragon is capable of sorting things out, even if it's difficult for her. Do you both understand what I'm saying?" She squeezed the girls' hands and smiled at them. Both granddaughters hugged their nan, she was such a good listener.

"Now Chesten, tell me all about this young lad, Jack."

"You'll see him tonight; he's coming to the meeting. I'm sure you'll like him."

Tamara picked up her sketch pad and started drawing. She didn't need or want to listen to this conversation. Phoebe noticed her dismissal of any news concerning Jack. *It was something the girl would have to cope with*, she thought.

"Nan," interrupted Tamara. "Can we hear about the disaster?"

Evasive action, thought Phoebe. *That's put an end to any talk about Jack.* She noted Tamara's cunning.

When Sam returned with the tea, Phoebe was about to begin her telling of the oil disaster.

"I know Sennen Cove is a cold place," joked Sam. "This should warm you up, and a cup of tea always goes down well with a story telling," he added, pouring Phoebe her first cup.

Phoebe grimaced at the joke. It was true, her cottage did take a lot of heating and was riddled with draughts, but she found herself unable to leave behind all of the happy memories that had built up there. They were sleeping in the stone walls, painted in layers on the old wooden doors, and when needed they could be called upon any time of the day or night. The cottage gave her comfort and enabled her to still feel close to her husband, Tom, who had died four years ago: he was in the very fabric of the place.

"Well girls," began Phoebe, who loved story telling time with her granddaughters. "We had been married a few months and were settling into our new home, the tumble-down cottage in Sennen Cove — of course you know it well. Tamara nodded and Chesten smiled — they both loved nan's cottage. "It was a thrilling time, full of new hopes and promises as only young newlyweds can appreciate. Tom would work the fishing boat all day and come home looking so healthy and happy, my heart would ache with the sight of him. We had put most of our money into the boat so that we would be able to generate a good living from it. We were being very sensible! *Pheebz,* the boat was named. Your grandad said one day we would have a fleet of fishing vessels: he had big dreams, as young people often do."

Tamara noticed the transition — from Tom to grandad. Her nan was fluid with her use of words to depict people. Or maybe it was intentional. It intrigued her how people held so many different titles: husband, grandad, father, son, Tom, friend, sailor... The various names portrayed different layers of a personality; they were subtly different but referred to the same person. Some people never noticed the differences, but she did. A certain curve of the lips to create a smile from a husband. An eyebrow raised in a quizzical manner from a father. An open demeanour from a friend. As an artist she studied these subtle mannerisms and tried to capture them in her drawings. Her sister was an interesting case to study — so many layers... Tamara let the notion go and settled down to listen to the story.

Phoebe drew breath and continued, "The tumble-down cottage was so quaint. We managed to get it at a very reasonable price. I don't think anyone else wanted it! Everything was perfect. We even named the cottage, "Tumble Down Cottage". They were good times. We believed that we were invincible and nothing would change, but that's not true. Nothing stays the same, everything changes, but of course we were much too young and naive to realise that." Phoebe paused to look at her granddaughters. As a good narrator she felt the need to check their interest in her stories. It was a habit she had developed during her time as a journalist: you needed to keep your audience interested. She hadn't lost the knack.

Chesten was hanging onto every word. She loved the part that described how much in love her nan and grandad had been as newlyweds and how thrilling their life together had been. It sounded idyllic, and she allowed herself a few moments to picture life with Jack, setting up home in Sennen Cove or Porthenby. Moving away from this part of the country wasn't in Chesten's plans, and she hoped Jack felt the same. It was just a dream.

Listening intently, Tamara urged the story onwards… to the sighting of the Dragon. She knew the Dragon would make an appearance. How could she not when a disaster loomed? Although she always demanded proof of her existence, before allowing herself to accept such fairy stories, Tamara had always nurtured a secret desire to believe in the Dragon. Today she had been provided with evidence; she had seen the Dragon. She was sure of it.

While she had been concentrating on Phoebe's story, Tamara had sketched the creature she had seen as it swam through the strait. Her sharp grey eyes, the colour of the wintry North Atlantic Ocean, could gauge scale and depth to an amazing degree. She was destined for art college, her teacher had informed Edith and Sam. Denying herself any use of colour had sharpened her perspective and allowed her imagination to run free, which was exactly what her art teacher said she needed to do. Although she had a talent that well exceeding her age, Tamara had yet to develop her style and struggled to allow her artist's impression to take over. She played safe, always producing excellent work and gaining top marks, nevertheless her art teacher knew she was capable of much more. She was pleased with this sketch and made a mental note to add it to her portfolio, which when presented to the Art College in Bristol would hopefully secure her a scholarship. It would be a wrench leaving the cove but a sacrifice she was willing to make in order to pursue her career. Maybe one day she would return to set up her art gallery, but first she would need to gain experience outside the cove. It was just a dream.

Phoebe leaned over to look at the drawing. “Exactly as I remember her.”

“Thanks, nan. I’m not quite sure about the size. Maybe she’s larger? Longer perhaps?”

“It all depends on how and where you see her. Sometimes she merges with the sea, and it’s difficult to grasp any concept of her size. At other times, when the sea is having a rest and the day is calm, you can gain quite a good idea of her true dimensions. Maybe her shape and size alter from day to day. Who knows? All I can say is that you have caught the quality of her.”

Phoebe drew breath and continued with her story. “It was the obnoxious smell, rolling in on the sea breeze, that presented itself first. It prepared the way for the oncoming disaster. At that time we hadn’t heard of the shipwreck, but we knew something dreadful must have happened. We made our way down to the beach, where people had gathered, and looked apprehensively out to sea. We stayed there all morning, feeling nauseous and anxious with the foul-smelling air circling around us, fighting the impulse to run away, choosing to stay and face whatever was going to appear. We were waiting for answers to all the questions buzzing around in our heads. The beach was packed with fishermen, local shop keepers, firemen, local councillors; all manner of people convened there, staring towards the horizon. We didn't know what to expect. It took a while for the oil to arrive on the coastline by which time everyone was aware of the oil tanker's fate — she had become speared by the jagged rocks lying around the cove and was impaled there. A wounded beast — frightened and dangerous. Toxic oil gushed from her damaged body as her life force faded away, and the winds and high spring tides rushed the poisonous oil towards our beaches. We saw the tanker's innards making their way towards us, slippery and shiny, weighing down the waves which rippled pathetically onto the shore. The sludgy brown mud was laid to rest on the shoreline. Beaches, coves and harbours all along the North Coast of Cornwall were decimated" Phoebe paused to collect her memories of that horrendous time. She shook her head and continued.

"Your grandad looked broken. He knew things were about to change drastically and not for the better. Being on the sea and earning a living from it had been in your grandad's blood since he was a little boy. He had often helped his grandad and father with their netting and from a young age was extremely adept and knowledgeable about the sea. He knew the North Cornwall coastline like the back of his hand. Achieving his ambition to own his own boat and carry on with the family tradition of fishing was a milestone in his life, but the future began to look precarious when the oil arrived. Devastated by the sights and smells on the beach we held hands and walked away from the catastrophe, towards our cottage. As we drew nearer, we saw swirls of colours dancing around on the sea-facing front windows of our home and exchanged puzzled glances. It wasn't until we were outside our garden gate that we realised what had happened. The oil had been blown inland and a fine film of it covered the cottage. The wind had continued with the gruesome game and chased the oil around the windows making grotesque patterns. Our front door handle was slimy and greasy to touch, it had become wrapped in a film of the filthy stuff, which made opening the door virtually impossible. It seemed as though the cottage needed to protect herself by not allowing the foul pollution to enter, but in doing so she was also turning her back on us as well as the happy memories we had started to build there."

"Oh nan, you must have been devastated," Chesten sighed.

Phoebe bit her bottom lip to prevent her voice from wavering, she needed to tell this story. "The pollution was everywhere. We needed to do something; be proactive, not give in. Your grandad and I weren't made that way: we would find a way forward. That night after tea, when we had drawn the curtains and settled down in front of the fire, we talked about how we would cope and what we would do. The conversation drifted towards the Porthenby Dragon. I knew your grandad was undecided about whether or not the Dragon was a reality, and I realised that it was time for me to tell him about my sightings and knowledge of her. Even though I trusted your grandad implicitly, it made me feel extremely vulnerable sharing my secret with him. What if he didn't believe me? How would we move forward from that point? I took the plunge and trusted in my instincts, knowing I had to share my secret with him if we were going to work together to save her. I suggested maybe it was time to seek her out — make sure she was able to cope with the enormous task of cleaning up the whole of North Cornwall's sea and beaches. Nothing of this magnitude had been seen before, and although I knew she was capable of amazing acts of redressing wrongs and balancing nature, maybe this time it would be too much for her to deal with, alone. Your grandad listened patiently while I recounted the times that I had seen the Dragon at Porthenby Island. He was enthralled, and my confidence grew as I began to realise he believed my stories. I told him about my sightings of the Dragon, which went back all the way to my childhood. He listened intently."

"How old were you when you first saw the Dragon?" Tamara asked.

"Not very old, perhaps ten or eleven. As a child, I often picnicked on Porthenby Island with my mum and grandma. They would entertain me with stories about the Dragon and that's all I imagined they were — stories, but I was wrong. It was on one of these occasions that I first saw her. It was at the beginning of the Easter holidays with no school for two weeks. All children love this time of the year, the beginning of spring and being able to spend time outdoors. I was looking forward to playing outside with my friends and being able to go on adventures with my mum. When she suggested we could go for a picnic on the island I was delighted, it was one of my favourite places, still is. Eagerly I helped her prepare the picnic, choosing lots of snacks that I liked: buns, cakes, lemon tarts. She always let me choose. My mum made her delicious raspberry jam sandwiches, smothered in butter; one of my favourite treats. It was going to be a child's feast. The day was one of those early spring surprises, mild with the sun shining down on the island, warming the air and clearing away the last of the winter chills.

"I remember grandma meeting us at the picnic site we had chosen. She looked lovely. Always dressed smartly, on that day she wore a beautiful cream lace outfit. Rather unsuitable for an outdoor picnic attire but totally grandma's style. I still have it today, and it fits me perfectly. It's funny the small things you remember as a child: the colour of a dress, the smile formed just for you, the delicious jam sandwiches only your mother could make. All the prompts that make recollection of childhood memories pleasant to saunter through.

"After we had finished our picnic, mum suggested we let grandma have a few minutes peace and quiet while we went to the bridge to watch the flood tide. Watching the incoming tide race through the strait and back out into the ocean was exhilarating and hypnotic, so I eagerly agreed. Mum smiled at grandma who acknowledged the gesture with an imperceivable nod. I looked at them both, and although I was confused as to what they were sharing I was preoccupied with making my way onto the bridge. I raced off, as fast as my young legs allowed, leaving mum far behind. I stood on the bridge, alone, looking down at the foamy energetic sea, feeling very brave with myself, as only a young child could. I wasn't afraid of the swaying bridge or the tumultuous sea. I felt defiant as I stood against the elements. Mum caught up with me, and we stood side by side while the waves hurled sea spray high into the air, which rained down gently and softly covering our faces. We both laughed out loud. There was nowhere else in the world I would rather have been: it was perfect.

"We hadn't been there for more than five minutes when I saw the Dragon, crashing around the rocks at the entrance of the strait. She was heading directly towards us. My heart was thumping in my chest. I must admit I was petrified. My mum held me in her arms to reassure me and told me the Dragon was nothing to be afraid of; she was there to do her job and wouldn't harm us. Mum explained to me that the Dragon enters the Mermaid Cave on the flood tide and rests there until she returns to the ocean depths on the ebb tide. While she rests in the cave her breath streams out of the blowing hole and penetrates the whole of the local area, helping to soothe wrongs and promote rights."

"Exactly what dad says," Tamara interrupted.

"It's the truth Tamara. Now that you've seen her, I'm sure you'll find it more believable," Phoebe said quietly.

"Shush Tammy, let nan tell her story."

Phoebe smiled at her granddaughters and continued with her story, "My mum explained that in the spring the Dragon encourages new growth. In the summer she motivates the crops to flourish and ripen. In the autumn she inspires the harvest to fruition and encourages animals to prepare for the long winter months. And in the winter... she allows the world to rest before it all begins again. It was a simple explanation for a child to understand, and one I think still holds true today. Mum said very few people could actually see the Dragon, although she knew I would be one of those... when the time was right.

"As the Dragon swam underneath the bridge, I couldn't believe the size of her, absolutely enormous and so beautiful — every shade of cyan you could imagine. I wasn't afraid anymore and stared, mesmerised by her magnificence. Instinctively I knew to keep my sighting a secret from my friends, they wouldn't believe me; I would be ridiculed. Mum said that was a sensible thing to do: people had difficulty believing in such things. We knew it to be true, so we could talk about it together, with grandma.

"I had a few sightings of the Dragon after that eventful day, always on the bridge on Porthenby Island. The Dragon never failed to enthral — she had captivated me with her beauty and strength. Mum said the Dragon was doing a fine job, everything was as it should be. I knew your grandad believed my story; he had heard about the

Dragon but had never seen her. Part of him had thought it was folklore, and part of him had thought it was true, which is the way of most Cornish folk. We decided that night to take two courses of action; one would be to call a meeting between local people to see what could be done to address the disaster, the other was to visit the Dragon to offer our help if she needed it."

"But nan," Tamara interrupted sharply, "you've always said to leave well alone. The Dragon would sort things out."

Chesten looked towards her nan, observing her reaction to Tamara's outburst, studying her body language for hidden clues.

"Well, it's difficult to explain. In our defence I can only say that we were young and foolhardy. Maybe it's also partly due to my nature, I always think I can control things, solve problems. We didn't have any clear plan in mind. At the time I felt the need to see her, so I could satisfy myself she was alive and well."

Tamara quietened down and allowed her nan to continue.

"Of course, with the scale of the disaster government officials stepped in. With my connections on the Kernow News I quickly arranged a meeting between the residents. Maybe together we could come up with ideas and strategies to help rid ourselves of the mess we were in. Lots of ideas were offered, some very practical and achievable. We realised our local knowledge of the sea and land needed to be shared with the committee of scientists and government officials, so we could work together and clear up the devastation. One suggestion that we made was to pump out the tanker. A few sailors had seen this done during the war, when fuel was transferred to destroyers and ships at sea, so they knew it was achievable. They volunteered to accompany the auxiliary tankers to offer their experience and expertise to the task. Our suggestion was refused on the grounds it was too dangerous. It seemed as if everything we proposed was dismissed; we felt surplus to requirements."

"How ridiculous! Why didn't they listen to the sailors?" Tamara demanded.

"It was a different time, Tamara. I'm sure the local voice would be heard now — and respected."

Chesten remained quiet, silently urging the story to continue.

"Working groups were set up by the locals in an attempt to try and clean up the beaches. We used buckets and mops; it was a mammoth task. Sea and bird life were hit cruelly. Fortunately, we managed to save some. We washed the oil from them and built temporary shelters until they were strong enough to survive in the wild. What else could we do? It was heartbreaking seeing birds deposited on the oil polluted beaches, struggling to stay alive. They were broken, and we tried our hardest to put the pieces back together. Rumours were bouncing around, no one knew what was true or false anymore. We heard that chemicals were going to be sprayed onto the oil in an attempt to disperse it, understandably we thought that couldn't be true. Surely chemicals would only make the situation worse!

"Disillusioned and exhausted, your grandad and I decided to visit Porthenby Island to see if the Dragon would reveal herself to us: maybe she held some answer to our problem. We needed to find a way forward out of the nightmare, so we took a leap of faith. We didn't go with any plan of action; we went because we were at a total loss of what to do next. The need to take some control back in our neighbourhood was growing amongst the community, perhaps your grandad and I could help. I knew we needed to be on the bridge when the tide turned, that's when we were most likely to see her on the incoming flood tide, when she would swim past us and into Mermaid Cave.

"Your grandad and I stood anxiously waiting for her arrival, it was early evening, and the light was beginning to fade. She appeared as soon as the tide turned and swam slowly towards us, no longer the fast, energetic, athletic beast I recalled as a child. She looked broken. Her red, irritated skin was visible with bare patches showing where her scales had sloughed off. As she looked up at me standing on the bridge, her eyes looked glazed and tired: yet I was sure that I saw a hint of recognition in them. She had obviously been working hard to try and repair the damage done by the oil and chemicals. The effect it had on her body was horrendous. Your grandad, clearly shaken, gasped at the sight of her. I wished his first sighting of her could have been when she displayed her full magnificence. However, now wasn't the time for sentimentality as action was needed, but how could we help her? She slid beneath us and despondently swam through the strait. Your grandad put his arm around me and told me not to worry. Everything was going to work out and would be fine."

"That sounds just like grandad," Chesten said, "he was always so positive."

Phoebe nodded in agreement saying, "I always felt we could achieve anything together; we made a good team, your grandad and I. After our sighting of the Dragon, we made our way onto the island and spread a blanket across the grass to eat the picnic we had prepared. Not having much of an appetite, we silently went through the motions of enjoying the food. The sun had set by this time, and a full moon cast its lustrous glow over the island, which had a surprisingly calming effect on both of us. Your grandad held my hand and promised he would fix our Dragon saying maybe she needed a little help. He was sure that together we would think of a way. I smiled at him, realising at that moment how much I loved him, he would do anything for me. I was very lucky to have him in my life. As I began to relax, we started to talk quietly about how we might be able to help the Dragon when suddenly your grandad put his fingers to his lips. He pointed over to the edge of the sea-facing cliffs and there they were — the loony moonies."

"It's what Tamara still calls them now," laughed Chesten.

"They are!" Tamara declared. "What kind of animal sits staring at the moon in deep meditation? Hares — loony moonies."

Phoebe sighed as the strange, mystical recollections of that evening swamped her. She allowed herself to ponder and gathered her composure before she continued. "The moonlight bathed the hares from top to toe in silvery light. As their ears twitched, we could see the brightness rippling along their length making them seem comically elongated — even for a hare. Staring hypnotically, not at the moon that night but at the blowing hole, the drove took on the appearance of being in deep meditation. Your grandad and I were captivated — it came to me that maybe they were acknowledging and worshipping the Dragon. The hares caused the night air to become charged with positive energy, I wondered if this was an attempt to help the Dragon repair herself. The Dragon's feeble breath, emerging from the blowing hole, caught the moonbeams and danced in the still night air. There was a magical quality at play that night: the still night air, glittering moonlight, hypnotic hares and the Dragon's breath. The combination was heady, and I felt tears running down my cheeks.

"The spell was broken by a few leverets breaking

away from the drove, they were bored with the silence and stillness as young creatures often are. The natural order of the night quickly resumed as they started play boxing, flexing their young muscles and strengthening their ligaments, preparing themselves for adulthood. A sea of flashing, glistening limbs against the backdrop of the dark Atlantic Ocean. It only lasted a few moments, and then they were sternly pulled back into the drove. They were severely reprimanded by their elders. The joint cognition had been lost and the hares, unable to resume their group performance, disbanded and went their own separate ways. I remember thinking how strange it was seeing so many hares together, being the solitary creatures they are, but then the whole scene was unreal. It seemed as if the elements were trying to console the Dragon, urging her on to continue with her task of setting things right. I wondered if she had the strength to succeed…"

As the kitchen clock struck the seventh hour, Phoebe noticed Chesten stir. She knew the girl would be apprehensive and excited at the prospect of Jack arriving for the meeting.

Phoebe whispered to her granddaughters, "I'll talk to you later girls, we have company now."

The Assembly

It was a congregation of anxious people who gathered together at Cove Cottage, to talk about their problems and unusual happenings, hoping there would be some plausible explanation and a quick resolution. The cottage walls seemed to take a deep breath, stretch and expand to accommodate the twenty or so people who crossed the threshold. Eyes darted around the room, searching the sea of faces in anticipation of finding a trickle of hope. The atmosphere was fragile, it needed tending with a soft voice and friendly demeanour. Edith Pascoe was perfect for the role. The aroma of percolating coffee drifted slowly from the kitchen warming the mood of the assembly, encouraging people to gather there — to relax and chat. Edith decided the best way forward for this meeting was to encourage informality. When people were at ease and formal barriers were dissolved, much more could be achieved… in her opinion.

Jack made his way into the living room in an attempt to find Chesten, and there she was, sitting on the chair arm next to her grandmother. She looked spectacular. Illuminated by the open fire her hair took on a life of its own, framing her beautiful pale face. Chesten stood up to greet him, and his heart melted. He loved this cottage, this family and of course Chesten. They had known each other since primary school, had even been in the same class. In those days, in an effort to control her hair, it had been plaited. This made it an easy target for some of the children, including himself, to give it a playful tug as they ran past her. She always laughed this off, staring at them with her sea green glare in quasi-annoyance. Maybe he had always been a little bit in love with her.

"Hi Jack! Would you like a tea, coffee? Or something stronger? Chesten asked teasingly.

Jack looked like a rabbit caught in the headlights. He glanced swiftly between Chesten and her grandmother. Surely, she couldn't be offering him a real drink, as in alcohol? Not in front of her grandmother.

Phoebe laughed at his expression, "Don't worry Jack, she's pulling your leg. Chesten, stop tormenting the boy, go and get him a drink. It's either tea or coffee… or hot chocolate!"

Chesten led Jack back into the kitchen and made her way towards the percolator, which was in a cosy niche near the open fire. The ideal place to stand, central to hear all the views of the people gathered there but slightly isolated from the assembly. With the excuse of making coffee, Chesten had removed herself and Jack from the main body of the meeting. Jack realised what she had done and was pleased.

The kitchen always seemed to be the natural meeting place for people and willingly accommodated them. The extension Sam had completed, a few years ago, quite happily served his growing family and the multitude of visitors it received. Cove Cottage was an open house, with people dropping in most days to chat and pass the time of day with Sam or Edith. It was a place where worries and reassurances could be shared.

The calming influence of the cottage, together with the homely smell of percolating coffee, began to work its magic on the assembly. People were beginning to unwind and loosen up in preparation for the meeting. Edith considered it an appropriate time to call the assembly together.

"Thank you everyone for attending our meeting. We will try to keep it as informal as we can. Most people will have something to say, so we need to give them some space and time to enable them to voice their concerns. Coming from all walks of life, with different perspectives, we all have valuable information to offer tonight, which we may be able to act upon. Some of us are more confident when speaking in public," Edith fixed a look at Major Rupert Angove who answered with a shrug of his shoulders. "We need to make this a safe place, so everyone feels able to offer an opinion, however outlandish it may seem. We won't learn anything if we all try to speak over each other; only if we listen can we learn. Would anyone like to start the meeting? Are there any concerns about happenings in or around Porthenby?" Edith smiled and looked around the room to see if anyone, who might feel uncomfortable about offering their opinion, needed her help to start the conversation.

"I can't say I've noticed anything out of the ordinary," boomed Major Angove, ignoring Edith and taking the lead in the assembly. Rupert Angove was a high-ranking official with the Ministry of Defence: he had worked there since the mid-nineties. His role, of late, was mainly as an ambassador for the Ministry, and as such he felt the need to attend local meetings to ensure any blame wasn't placed directly at his door, which it often was. The list of complaints he could recall was endless: rumours circulating about munitions from WW2 being dumped out at sea, gas cylinders from WW1 buried underground, the adverse effect caused by the spraying of chemicals during the oil disaster, you name it and the MoD was to blame. By commencing the debate (as he considered it to be) it gave him the upper hand. Better to attack than be on the defence. He always loved a good debate and was known locally for his fiery, passionate speeches about the Protection of the Peninsula (Cornwall). His heart was in the right place, but sometimes his ideas needed soothing and modifying and who better to do that than Edith? With her quiet reasonable ways, she could often lead him into considering, if not accepting, a different point of view. At times he would come across as stubborn and arrogant, although close friends knew it was a defensive front he had built up over the years. A survival tactic he probably needed with the circles he moved in.

"Thank you, Rupert," Edith interrupted, knowing Rupert was about to launch into his spiel about any problems having nothing to do with the MoD. "We're not here to apportion blame, simply to determine if we have a problem in Porthenby. So… we need to listen to everyone's feelings and experiences." Edith hoped he would settle down, now that he had heard his own voice, and allow other members of the assembly to gather their thoughts and confidence to talk. People needed to share their ideas without being bullied or ridiculed.

Fly Away Peter, Fly Away Paul

Sergeant Harry Dyer began his address. He was the retired local policeman, and one of the more confident members of the assembly. Edith was pleased he had taken the initiative to be the first speaker. Being a down to earth character who was highly respected in the community, he would hopefully set the scene for the meeting. It would placate the assembly after Rupert's outburst.

"A couple of weeks ago, I took my birds to the spring meeting, the one near Land's End. After the winter months, with the pigeons mainly flying locally, I think it's important they take part in this meeting as it stretches their wings and helps to build up their muscle tone. It's a good flight, not too difficult, with enough distance to tax their homing instincts and help build up their flock loyalty. They always enjoy this first flight of the season."

"I always mark that date in my diary," Old Ben chortled. "It's a real pleasure to see the birds flying over my cottage on their way home. Marks the beginning of spring for me."

Voices of acknowledgment rippled through the assembly; Harry drew breath to continue.

"I chose my birds carefully, taking six of the fittest most experienced birds that I knew wouldn't get into difficulty. Knowing every aspect of the terrain from Land's End to Porthenby and being strong enough to make the flight, I wasn't concerned about their ability to make their way home. In fact, I was confident they would do it in record time. They had flown together on numerous occasions and had built up a flock familiarity. If any one of them encountered trouble, such as which direction to take or how high to fly, they would put their trust in the lead bird and follow them. My birds are very sociable, and they help each other — just like a family. Most importantly they all have a love of home, so I knew they would be eager to return there."

Spending many years of his life building up a good breeding stock of homing pigeons, Harry was respected amongst the pigeon fraternity for his knowledge and understanding of bird behaviour. He was a kind man and always treated his pigeons with love and respect, subsequently they responded and developed the "love of home", which Harry always declared was his magic ingredient. When he flew the birds, he knew the main thing on their minds was to return back to their roost as fast as their wings could carry them. They were well fed, fit and prepared for flight. He loved to watch as they demonstrated their prowess of the skies. His were the eager ones that would fly high when they were first released, drawing circles in the sky and studying the terrain. Remaining in a tight flock, they quickly picked up their bearings by working together as a team and communicating in their magical, long-established ways. Eager to start their journey a leader would emerge, and the flock would follow. Their homing memory was excellent, and they would swiftly and surely take the safest most direct route back home. He would be waiting anxiously to clock them in. Although he believed in their ability, it was still an apprehensive time, like watching a toddler taking their first tentative steps — you prepared yourself to catch them if they stumbled.

His first sighting of the lead bird would dispel any

doubts about their safety, and the tension would be released from his body. Every flight offered something new, and he would watch with delight as his flock swiftly winged their way home. Carefully checking the birds in and noting their flight times, Harry would feel the swell of pride begin to surge as he knew, yet again, his birds had won the race even before the winner was declared. The birds were the champions of the county, winning far too many competitions for his rivals' liking. Some say the Racing Homer (a specific breed of pigeon used for the sport) that was in Harry's school, had descended from the homing pigeons used to carry messages in the First World War. Being the fine specimens they were, it was probably true.

People listened quietly as Harry Dyer shared his story. A few had heard about the incident when it had happened but not everyone was aware, so they respectfully paid attention, allowing him to continue.

"On the day of the first flight of the season I met with the South West Kernow Racing Pigeon Club. It was good to meet up with old friends and chat about our pigeons. We always have plenty of advice to offer each other, particularly on the first meeting after the long winter months. We chatted about everyday pigeon news such as new recipes we were feeding our flocks, any alterations to living conditions that were considered to be more favourable, all the stuff we loved to chat about for hours on end but bored most people."

Old Ben laughed out loud at this comment, "I've never found it boring."

Harry smiled at him and continued, "We all released our birds at noon, at the Land's End site, and saw them rapidly gain height, aided by the warm air currents. The conditions were perfect for a first flight of the season. I took comfort from this as I'm usually quite nervous at this point with questions buzzing around my head — how long will they circle, when will they start to head home, which bird will lead?

"Surprisingly, Peeky, my blue and white boy quickly took the lead. I knew that was unusual as Wilson, being a few seasons more experienced, usually took the lead, particularly on the first flight of the season. They were all excellent birds, every one of them capable of leading but, over time, Wilson had gained the flock's trust and had emerged as their leader — until that day. He seemed quite content with the decision and fell into line, allowing Peeky to take his place; maybe it was time to hand over the reins to new blood. Pigeons always surprise you, there's always something new to learn about them. I remember someone in the club, I think it was Tim Meadows, saying it was unusual for Peeky to lead. I said that possibly he was becoming more comfortable with the flock and that a new hierarchy was developing; he certainly ticked all the boxes for the job. I stood there anxiously watching my birds and saw them fly out over the ocean, which was an unusual choice of route for them but still acceptable. Quite feasibly my new leader was trying out a different route, putting his stamp on the flock, even though the fastest route was overland. I reasoned that this time I wouldn't win the race, but at least Peeky would have gained valuable experience as the dominant bird. I was eager to get home, so I could get my pigeons into their loft and check them over. Thankfully, Mabel would be there to clock them in when they arrived because they would fly home faster than I could travel by car. Being married for over forty odd years, Mabel knew all about racing pigeons. How could she avoid it? Still… I was eager to see them myself."

A few members of the assembly laughed at this

comment. They had heard Mabel moan, on quite a few occasions, about having to stay at home to clock the birds in when she would rather have been somewhere else.

"Mabel knew how important it was to enter their details when they arrived home, so I could check it against their personal best and as undisputable proof of their flight times. I quickly said goodbye to my pals from the club and headed home. When I arrived, I went straight down to the pigeon loft: as much as they loved Mabel, they would want to see me. From Mabel's expression I knew something was wrong; things weren't right. She told me Wilson had arrived home, a little later than expected, but the rest were still out there. I told her Peeky had taken the lead and probably got lost taking the rest of the flock with him. Wilson must have broken away from them and made his own way home. What other explanation was there? But why hadn't the flock followed Wilson when they had obviously hit trouble? Things weren't right, I couldn't find any answers to the questions I kept asking myself. We waited up all night for the birds to return, sadly we haven't had a sighting to this day. It's never happened before; I can't explain it. Something is wrong."

The room was silent; no one knew what to say. It was obvious Harry was deeply upset about his pigeons, and the situation was made worse by the fact that it remained a mystery. Until it was solved, he wouldn't be able to find any peace.

"I'm sorry to hear about your birds, Harry," Edith said in an attempt to break the strained atmosphere in the room. "We are here tonight to try to find answers, and hopefully we will be able to spill some light on this mystery."

The Porthenby Crab

Looking around the room, Edith noticed Eleanor Teague who was trying, unsuccessfully, to contribute her news to the assembly. Being of a quiet and timid disposition, Edith knew she would need to pave the way for her. Edith admired the meticulous precision of Eleanor's work, if anyone found something out of the ordinary it would be her.

Eleanor had taken it upon herself to monitor the rock pool life around Porthenby for quite a number of years. Rumour had it that as a young girl she had been devastated by the sterility of the rock pools after the oil disaster and had decided to monitor their progress, at three monthly intervals, in the hope of seeing new life emerge. She had mountains of records, which tracked the progress of life forms that had re-established themselves in the pools. Eleanor stated that if the rock pools were healthy and supporting life then everything was on an even keel: they mirrored the well-being of the surrounding land and sea.

"Eleanor, it's nice to see you here tonight. Would you like to tell the assembly about any unusual happenings you may have noticed in Porthenby?" encouraged Edith.

Eleanor, who was clearly agitated, began her account. "When I did my quarterly inspection of the rock pools, a couple of days ago, to check on the diversity of the pool population, I was devastated to find the Porthenby crab had disappeared. I couldn't find one."

"Could you explain a little more?" coaxed Edith. "Maybe some natural predator has gained entry to the rock pools?

The room remained silent, waiting for Eleanor to compose herself and continue.

"That's what it is!" interrupted Rupert. "Some natural predator has been introduced to the rock pools. Stands to reason, it's the natural course of things."

"What do you think, Eleanor?" Edith enquired softly, trying to ignore Rupert's brash tone which she knew would unsettle Eleanor. "Could it be natural predators?"

"Anything's possible," confirmed Eleanor, "but I'm sure I would have noticed a new predator in the pools, particularly one that would endanger the Porthenby crab. I've seen first-hand, through monitoring the rock pools, how nature cleanses and regenerates itself. It's amazing, all it needs is time and patience. The desire to interfere must be curbed… leave well alone," Eleanor began to drift off into her peculiar, trance like way of talking which tended to unnerve most people. Anna, her sister, held her hand in an attempt to quieten her and bring her back from wherever she dwelled; it didn't work. "As in the case of the oil disaster. If the Dragon had been left to deal with the problem, without human interference, then it wouldn't have been so dire. She could have coped with the oil, but when the chemicals were piled on top of it… she must have been overwhelmed. Heaven knows how she managed to clear all the mess!" Eleanor was clearly becoming more distressed, but she needed to say what was troubling her, "And now… something's happening again, in the sea around Porthenby, causing the rock pools to become unstable. If you want my opinion, this doesn't seem like a natural occurrence. As I've already said I would have noticed any new predators."

Murmurs of agreement flowed through the room.

Everyone knew how efficient Eleanor was with her observations and recordings. If there were any new predators in the pools, she would have spotted them and recorded them. So, what had happened to the crabs?

"Hold on a minute," interrupted Simon Genn, who ran the local post office. "We're here tonight to discuss problems in Porthenby, not some fairy tale about a dragon!"

The room went silent as people either acknowledged or dismissed the idea of the Dragon being a reality. Most people accepted the inclusion of the Dragon being in every day talk or chat, they didn't hold any strong convictions about whether she was a myth or reality. Some people smiled when she was mentioned, saying that it was probably a sighting of a large seal plus an overactive imagination. Others said that maybe a few too many drinks in The Mermaid's Retreat also contributed to the stories of her existence. One or two locals were more adamant in their views and fervently denied her existence, ridiculing any believers. Edith noticed a few members of the assembly felt uncomfortable when the Dragon was mentioned. She understood that not everyone believed in her existence, but she hoped they would decide to stay and support the assembly. In a crisis, such as this, everyone needed to pull together not fight amongst each other. Edith noticed a few dismissive, shaking heads as people began to gather up their belongings, preparing to leave. Simon and Megan Genn were part of this group as they were staunch disbelievers in the local folklore and didn't entertain any fanciful ideas about dragons.

Harry Dyer jumped in to placate the meeting. "You've done a brilliant job, Miss Teague. Facing all kinds of weather, maintaining mountains of documentation, never missing an inspection date. If anyone is an expert on rock pool life in Porthenby, it's you!"

"Thank you, Sergeant Dyer," blushed Eleanor.

"We'll get to the bottom of where the Porthenby crabs have disappeared to," added Edith. "Maybe one or two local people would be willing to help Eleanor with her paperwork or take part in the inspections?" Edith directed her question towards Simon and Megan, who were still wondering whether to leave or stay. If they decided on the former then a few other members may also choose to join them, and she wasn't about to lose anyone from the audience, not without a fight. In Edith's experience fervent deniers often sought support in order to reinforce their own convictions. They persistently chipped away at others' beliefs and ideas or chose to ridicule statements that conflicted with their own, constantly trying to convince other people, and themselves, they were right. There wasn't room for negotiation or any acceptance of a different perspective, they were right and others were wrong. Edith needed to defuse this situation and bring some control to the meeting.

"A database perhaps? It could throw some light on the disappearance of the crabs." Edith smiled at Simon and Megan, as she tried to warm the conversation. "Simon, I know you are an expert with computers. Could you help out with this?"

All eyes were on Simon, who was visibly flattered and bathed in the glory of the compliment, much to the annoyance of his wife. Sitting up straighter, he was pleased to be the centre of attention, eagerly committing to a day a week helping Eleanor with setting up a database for the rock pools. The assembly gradually settled down to address the problem again. Everyone stayed. Edith could charm the ducks off the water if she set her mind to it.

"Hasn't the Porthenby crab recently made an

appearance again, after being wiped out by the disaster?" interrupted Tamara.

"Yes," confirmed Eleanor, "you're right. It's been three years now since I first saw it reappear. I was over the moon to see it again, after such a long time. Its numbers have gradually increased, and things were looking pretty good for the little chappy. I never imagined that I'd see the crab again in our rock pools, not in my lifetime. It's a statement to the fact the seas around here are clean and healthy… but that's changing. In my opinion there's something wrong with the sea, something is working against nature and polluting it. The tiny crab is such a sensitive creature, it's one of the first to be affected when some unbalance of nature occurs — I'm worried about what or who will be affected next."

The silence in the kitchen was solid and impenetrable, preventing anyone from speaking and allowing them to consider the facts for a moment…

Mutton Cove

After the silence melted away and opinions started to be voiced, Jasper Lee decided to add his account, "I had a phone call this morning, from The National Trust."

The assembly settled down to listen to Jasper, who had been wondering about whether to contribute to the assembly with this news... whether or not it was relevant.

"They needed my help and advice on what to do over at Mutton Cove. As you know I've often been over there when problems occur: it's just another pair of hands to help out in a crisis." Every member of the assembly responded in agreement with Jasper, they knew not to contradict him, he was a humble man; forever underrating himself. But who else would they call if they had a problem with the seal sanctuary? It was common knowledge the Lee family had an understanding of animals. It was also known that Jack's father could be relied upon to help out in any situation that involved difficulty or trouble with animals.

"Steve, our local vet, was also called in to make sense of the situation. I've helped him on a few occasions, we have a good working relationship." Jasper paused to gather his thoughts. "I arranged to meet Steve at St Ives, where his boat is moored. As I arrived, Steve was loading the boat with medication and equipment that he thought we might need. He filled me in on what was happening. Apparently, a few of the seals didn't seem to be moving. This had been reported by a couple of tourists who were quite concerned. They had been watching the seals for a few hours and hadn't seen any signs of life. That's not unusual in itself, as they do swim into the secluded cove to seek shelter and peace. Most of the visitors respectfully acknowledge this and, by keeping noise to a minimum, they allow the seals to catch up on their forty winks."

This last statement caused a ripple of laughter to flow through the assembly. Most of them had been to Mutton Cove to view the seals from the headland, it was a unique experience. Looking down on the seals as they lolled around on the beach and rocks, relaxing and sunning themselves, it was hard to imagine a better way to spend a few quiet hours. They looked so chilled out that it made people take stock of their own lives and for a short time they emulated the seals' aura. It was as beneficial as a day out at the spa, Jasper had heard one tourist state.

"As most of you know the easiest way to access the cove is by boat, and as we approached quite a few of the seals took umbrage at our intrusion, pointedly making their way into the water. Being naturally shy creatures, we expected this. Steve and I laughed at their departure and announced to the seals that we wouldn't stay long on their beach; they could return soon. We noticed about half a dozen remained on the beach, they were pups and should have followed their elders into the ocean: learning by example. They appeared to be asleep, but we knew our presence would have disturbed them; they should be awake and alert. Both of us feared that something was drastically wrong for the seals to remain. It was with a heavy heart that I knelt down to examine the first cub. It was dead. Life had scarcely left its body. I felt disheartened for not arriving sooner, maybe I could have helped. Steve examined the cub from head to toe, but there were no outward signs of disease or damage; it didn't have a mark on its body. It looked healthy, a perfect specimen.

"We examined the five remaining seal pups: they too were dead. We racked our brains but couldn't think of any explanation that could have caused their death. I'm still puzzling over it now, there's no sense to it. We loaded the dead pups onto Steve's boat and took them back to his surgery where we will be able to examine them in more detail, maybe understand what has happened. If we don't solve this problem then the other members of the colony may succumb to the same fate as the pups."

"Such terrible news," Liz Rowe broke the silence in the room. "I hope you work out what has happened to the pups."

"When will you and Steve have any results?" Edith asked in a despondent manner. "This needs to be addressed as quickly as possible."

"Probably a couple of days. I'll let you know as soon as I can."

"Thank you, Jasper."

"It may be a shot in the dark but could there be any leakage, from the old munitions dump? The one that's situated in the abandoned tin mine near the old airbase," queried Sam. "I've heard there may be a runoff from the site into the sea. Maybe it could have affected the seals."

"Certainly not!" affirmed Rupert.

The Inspection

Major Angove was adamant that his voice would be heard, he needed to set the record straight. He had a feeling this meeting would result in blame being placed at his door.

"I don't know how many times we've been through this scenario. "Yes, there are munitions buried deep underground in the old tin mine up at the airbase. As you realise, decisions were made at the time, and they needed to be made quickly. It was shortly after the Second World War, with the country eager to move forward into peace time. The armaments needed to be stored away safely and effectively. My grandfather, who was in charge of the disposal, told me all the details. Where it's situated, how the weapons are stored. It's all perfectly safe. There's nothing there that could break or leak into the water table to pollute the rivers or seas. My father, who worked for the local Water Authority, always checked on this site, to ensure it remained safe. The armaments had to be disposed of somewhere, and that was the safest place available at the time. Where else would they go?"

A few members of the assembly were visibly shaking their heads, they obviously disagreed with the decision that had been taken years ago.

Harry Dyer decided to step in and reaffirm the safety of the post war decision. "I can vouch for that. It's all perfectly safe. I've been invited to accompany inspections of the tin mine with Major Angove and his colleagues."

A few select, respected members of the local community had been invited on these inspections. The idea was to reassure the neighbourhood of the consignment's safe storage.

"Everyone trusts the judgement of the local policeman," joked Harry, who realised he had been chosen to be part of the inspection team in order to offer credibility to the task. "As far as I could see everything seemed in order. Eleanor, you attended one of the inspections with me, and we both agreed everything was safely stored."

Eleanor mumbled her acknowledgement as memories of the inspection seeped into her mind. She drifted away from the hubbub of the meeting and reluctantly started to relive the distressing experience.

Deep in the disused tin mine, the underground storage room was low ceilinged and stuffy. Metal boxes were piled up high against white concrete walls, which were the colour of bleached bones. The air inside the tomb, as Eleanor considered it to be, was fetid which suggested that water had crept in… somehow. It caused her to retch. She tried to restrain herself, so that the others wouldn't notice her behaviour and call off the inspection, fearing she was having a panic attack. Eleanor was aware that some of the local people thought she was strange, somehow different from them. After overhearing a couple of older residents refer to her as "Eccentric Eleanor" she didn't want to reinforce that opinion by being the cause of a terminated inspection.

Her imagination ran riot, like a tsunami destroying everything in its path, which caused her to sink into deep dark notions concerning the history of the munitions. Flashes of horrendous wartime combat flooded into her mind, swamping her. She was there amongst the fighting: the threatening report of the rifles, burning buildings emitting their acrid smell, smoke billowing up and bleeding into the blue sky. She could feel the smooth, cold metal of the bayonet as it was fixed into place and the taste of fear was on her tongue. It was so vivid she could almost call it memory, but it couldn't be, she had never experienced first-hand combat in her life.

In the midst of chaos and horror which drenched her mind, a small trickle of hope swam against the current, gaining momentum drip by drip: determined to be heard. A young child, a girl, she had been saved by the rifle. It had been used to free her and cast peace around her. Eleanor was able to grasp hold of the concept, calm herself, rationalise her reasoning. It wasn't the armaments that were evil but the ideas and actions of some people. That was the problem, but how could she help solve it?

Eleanor was unable to concentrate on the inspection and was relieved when she emerged from the old tin mine and gasped her first breath of fresh Cornish air. Tranquillity gently flowed over her as she felt the freedom of the outdoors. Retelling her experience to her best friend and confidante, her sister, she had to agree with Anna's explanation that it was community memory playing tricks with her mind. Anna said that Eleanor had heard so many wartime stories, from various people, that now they had become her own memories. Eleanor accepted her sister's version of events and felt somewhat relieved, but still… it had seemed so real at the time.

Eleanor had always been a sensitive child, often crying when other children were hurt as if she endured their broken bones or cut knees herself. As an adult, her senses were still attuned to people's sorrows, failures and even memories. She was like a radio picking up human signals; their cries for help. How she wished she could soak up their happiness, pleasure and achievements, deny access to the sorrowful events, but this didn't seem to be her destiny. At times it was too much for her to cope with, and in an attempt to soothe her sister's troubled mind Anna would offer some plausible explanation. What would she do without her?

"Eleanor, are you alright?"

Eleanor was jolted back to the present by Anna, who was looking at her quizzically.

"Stop worrying about the Genns, they always dismiss any ideas which don't match their own. There are plenty of other people here who respect your opinions."

Eleanor wasn't concerned about the Genns, but she decided not to burden her sister with her flashback. She became aware of the room again and of Edith talking…

"I'm sure you're right Rupert," acknowledged Edith. We know from the regular inspections that the armaments are safely secured. Maybe you could offer some suggestions?" She didn't want this assembly to be about who was to blame, it was about working together.

Eleanor was back in the present, here and now. She waited a while, wondering what Rupert… and his friends, might suggest.

The Abandoned Undersea Tin Mine

Eleanor didn't have to wait long. Sam decided it was time to offer his childhood story but needed to include his friends in the telling.

"What about the old tin mine over Botack way? The mine that runs under the seabed for over a kilometre. We went there once when we were kids, even though our parents had warned us to keep away. It was dangerous, but we couldn't resist the adventure. You must remember… Rupert, Jasper?"

All three men looked at each other as they started to visualise the events of that horrendous day. It had started with a dare and had become a reality. They had been young boys, and the lure of danger was a novelty for them. It was rumoured, but never officially confirmed, that the old mine had been used as a site to store unused toxic gas from the First World War. At the time of the operation, people had said it was a deadly pioneering concoction that had never been used. No one knew its capabilities.

"I think we need to know more about this tin mine," coaxed Edith. She was aware of it but had never heard this story before. She wondered where it would lead and why Sam had never mentioned this childhood adventure to her.

As usual Rupert took the lead. "My grandfather, Major George Angove, often told stories about the old site. The mine had been closed a few years before the First World War was declared. It was considered a safe place to store the toxic gas that needed to be disposed of after the Great War: the war to end all wars," he added bitterly. "The consignment was sealed in metal tanks and taken into the mine via the entrance at Botack Headland. The knowledge and expertise of the local men who had worked there was sought because they knew its configuration and would be able to advise exactly where to store the load safely. One mistake and the outcome would have been catastrophic… for the whole of the local community."

At the time of the manoeuvre, that had aimed at being hush-hush, the news had travelled throughout the cove like greased lightning. However, that's where it ended… and stayed — in the cove. Porthenby was good at keeping secrets. The story had been handed down through the past few generations. Some members of the assembly were acknowledging the decision, which had been made over a hundred years ago, as being acceptable and realistic. Where else could the consignment have been stored? Others were quite vocal in their anger at the bygone decision, calling it reckless and stupid.

Rupert stood up straighter, looking around the assembly in an arrogant manner, causing the crowd to silence before he continued, "It was a long, arduous journey into the mine, carrying the awkward heavy tanks one at a time. It took the men several days to complete because they had to work in an extremely confined space and needed to handle the volatile consignment carefully. Once on site, the tanks were checked for stability; nothing was left to chance. The temperature in the mine would remain a steady constant, so everything was safe and secure for them to be housed there: they were in the most suitable place. At the end of the operation, the area was sealed off from the rest of the mine with a sturdy steel door fixed for access in the future, if ever it was needed. And that was the end of the matter. The gas had been safely stored without one person suffering any kind of injury. My grandfather was pleased with the outcome, but due to the secrecy of the mission he was never publicly acknowledged. He was advised to forget the matter, leave it to fade away, allow memory to dwindle over time. Obviously, that was never going to happen, you all know what collective memory is around these parts! Quite a few of the locals said it would be safe because the Dragon would ensure none of the gas would seep out and if it did, she would deal with it. My grandfather was adamant it was safe as long as it was left alone."

"Left alone!" shouted an angry voice from the back of the room. "That consignment should never have been dumped there in the first place. Your grandfather put everyone's life at risk."

"The gas should never have been produced in the first place, then we wouldn't have been faced with the difficulty of its disposal. Who on earth would invent such a deadly potion? They must have had a screw loose!" Another backroom voice shouted out, adding to the impending disruption of the meeting.

"You need to remember those actions were taken over a hundred years ago, a very different time from today. I've often considered the reasoning behind the decision to store the gas there, but unless you were present in that time and place, with the information available to you at that moment, it's difficult to follow any line of reasoning and pass judgement. Hindsight is a wonderful thing. As for the decision to produce the gas… it's a balance of power. If the enemy have it and you also have it, the two cancel each other out — everyone remains safe. It's too dangerous to use, knowing that your enemy could retaliate with the same deadly weapon." Rupert was growing tired of this argument and threw up his hands in despair.

Edith stepped in as the voice of reason, saying, "We need to listen to this story, it may have some relevance on our present situation. We've heard from Rupert the gas wasn't dumped! Using emotive language, such as that, inflames the situation. Also throwing accusations and family insults around isn't going to help anyone. Moral norms and accepted practices have changed considerably over the past hundred years. Futile attempts to apportion blame years after the incident is pointless. The past is there to learn from."

"Remember … we were young, silly daredevils," Sam jumped in, hoping the assembly would settle down to dealing with the present instead of blaming the past. "One day, during the long summer holidays from school, Rupert decided to tell the story concerning the old undersea tin mine, and the three of us became fired with a sense of adventure. We had heard rumours about the mine, but now we knew the facts the secret took on a life of its own: we needed to feed our curiosity… we wanted to see where the gas was stored."

"I'm not sure who suggested it, but the dare to enter the mine was set, we were all keen to get on with it," Jasper added, actively drawing people back into the story. "We set off there and then, as the ebb tide was on the turn, taking the short cut across the beach knowing Botack Cove was accessible at low tide. As we climbed up the steep cliffs from the cove towards the headland my sense of adventure was beginning to wane. I didn't expect that we would be able to enter the mine. Knowing it had been sealed I assumed our adventure would end at the entrance."

"I remember feeling quite relieved when we did reach the entrance and found it still locked," Rupert confessed. "Realistically, I knew it would be, but a nagging doubt had been tormenting me as I visualised the mine open to us. I feigned disappointment, so that I wouldn't be thought of as a coward."

"I felt the same," admitted Sam. "But annoyingly Jasper started to work away at the lock. He pulled it, pushed it, hit it with a rock. I wished he would leave it alone; we could find a better game to play. After a short time, the lock gave way."

"I was surprised when that happened," admitted Jasper. "Believe me, I didn't want the lock to break. I just wanted to appear brave and reckless! What had started off as an adventure was fast becoming a nightmare. We didn't know how to get out of it. No one wanted to appear cowardly. As Sam says we were young and silly."

"It shouldn't have broken so easily," continued Sam. "On numerous occasions kids had tried to gain entry to the mine, as kids do… yet the lock always held."

"I've often wondered about that myself," agreed Jasper.

"It was probably because the three of you were together," Eleanor offered. She believed the boys had greater strength when they worked together but decided to keep this opinion to herself.

Rupert looked quizzically at Eleanor, waiting for further explanation, but none came.

"Whatever forces were in play that day we should have told someone about what we found, but we were kids and scared of getting into trouble with our parents. We had been strictly forbidden to go anywhere near the mine, let alone to enter it," Sam declared. "Time passed, we all got on with our lives, and the adventure faded from our memories. After that day we didn't talk about it, not even with each other. Seems silly now but children think in different ways from adults. I'm sure everyone here has some secret they've kept from their parents!"

Rupert laughed and continued with the story, "The three of us looked at each other wondering what to do next. I'm not sure who took the lead, but we found ourselves squeezing past the metal door and stepping cautiously into the tunnel; the entrance to the mine. We had passed the point of no return. Someone suggested we take stock of any equipment we had with us which could be useful — boys of that age always have pockets stuffed with survival tools."

Tamara wandered over towards Chesten and Jack. She needed to be nearer her sister as this story unfolded. They both greeted her with a warm smile and made a Tamara-size space for her to stand in.

"It was dark, a darkness that wrapped itself around you," Sam declared. "As I peered into the mine it seemed to go on forever. The last vestiges of any sense of adventure drained from my body. I must admit I wanted to turn around and scurry away."

"Me too, every fibre of my body warned me not to enter the mine, but I couldn't lose face in front of both of you," Jasper declared. "My offering was my new torch, a birthday present that I carried around everywhere."

"I had some string and chuckstones," laughed Sam. "I didn't know what we were going to do with my collection, but at the time it seemed a good contribution."

"Chalk was my offering!" roared Rupert. "I thought we could mark our way along the passage as we walked through, then we would be able to find our way back to the entrance. Rather like Hansel and Gretel."

Jasper picked up the story, "We made a decision to walk through the mine until we came to the first junction in the tunnel, that's as far as we would go. If we hadn't located the storage area by then we would turn back. We reasoned that if we wandered around the mine, we would probably lose our way, and we weren't that silly… or brave. We talked about the ventilation down there, not understanding it but realising the air quality might become a problem the further we entered into the mine. It also provided a good excuse for us to turn back when we reached the first junction; a smokescreen to hide the fact that we were too afraid to venture further!"

"It was the smell I noticed first, old fetid air… air that hadn't seen the light of day for decades," Sam stated.

"I took the lead because I had the torch. Rupert wanted to lead, with my torch, but I wouldn't let him. We had a bit of a squabble, like most boys do."

"If we hadn't got that torch then we wouldn't have been able to proceed," Rupert said. "I remember thinking that if I dropped it and it broke, then we could turn back and find some other game to play. We could all save face. Sorry Jasper, I know that torch was your pride and joy."

"That's OK, Rupert. It was a good strategy, but unfortunately you didn't get the chance to carry it out. I wish you had. After our squabble Rupert backed down while I took the lead. He followed, marking crosses on the walls which were damp, making the task pointless as the chalk quickly washed away. We walked in single file because the passageway was quite narrow."

"We were all jumpy as we trudged down the steep incline of the mine. As you know, the tin mine runs under the seabed, and we became increasingly aware that we were walking or rather scrambling down to sea level," Sam continued, visibly shuddering. "I stretched my arms up and could nearly touch the top of the passage. Being closed in caused me to feel extremely anxious, and my heart began to pound in my chest. As we negotiated the slope the dampness intensified. Jasper's torch beam swept across our path, scanning the concrete walls and highlighting the glistening moisture resting there. I wished we had never started out on the adventure," Sam admitted.

"I'm sure that we all felt the same," sighed Rupert, "but we had gone too far with the dare. It had been agreed we make it to the first junction and no one wanted to back out."

"As the incline levelled out, we knew that we were below sea level, actually walking under the ocean. I could hear boulders being dragged along the seabed, constantly moving around by the force of the ocean," Sam continued. "They were unbelievably loud, as if they were only a few metres away, which they probably were. Jasper shouted that he could see the junction ahead. I felt relieved, thinking it wouldn't be long before we turned back."

"Searching the area with my torch to gather my bearings, I scrutinised the walls for any signs of openings or junctions. There was a road running straight on and one that turned to the right," Jasper recounted. "I could see and hear water running down the walls which was terrifying. I imagined the sea crashing through the walls and drowning us. Sam and Rupert were staring at a part of the wall where my torch beam had settled. As I dared myself to look closer I saw what they were focussing on… a crack in the wall. It shouldn't have been there."

"Tons of reinforced concrete had been used to make the walls of the mine safe before the gas was sealed in," Rupert explained. "My grandfather told me nothing would be able to get into the mine or out of it; it was a secure place to store the tanks. Yet there it was, staring us in the face: the outside coming in."

Sam drew breath to continue, "The sea water was

trickling into the mine through the fissure. To my terrified eyes it appeared to be pouring in. At that moment Jasper's torch flickered, and the light faded. Since his birthday he had been using it constantly, so the battery had drained. Rupert said we needed to get out of the mine before the torch died on us. As the words left his mouth the torch flickered and stopped working. We all gasped, we were frozen to the spot. I've never known such darkness. It penetrated every part of my body. I couldn't see my friends; I couldn't see anything. Panic surged through my body as the blackness enfolded me, it was choking and suffocating. The noise of the boulders dragging along the seabed grew louder and louder as if some even greater force had disturbed them. I tried to reason with myself that maybe the tide was on the turn, or perhaps a storm was building up. The thunderous noise was all-consuming which prevented me from thinking clearly. I was unable to concentrate on anything but the threatening proximity of the sea. I imagined it gushing through the walls, into the mine, sweeping me along passageways and into the depths of the tunnels. Leaving me floating around in icy cold salt water for eternity. I tried desperately to listen for any sounds from Rupert or Jasper to locate where they were, but it was impossible. I reached my hands out and tried to search for my friends, I needed their contact. That's when I felt a hand touch mine, and I grabbed it. The hand was warm and reassuring, it squeezed mine eagerly. I pulled Rupert towards me; I knew it was him. Asking where Jasper was, I felt rather than saw him shake his head. We had found each other, but where was Jasper?"

"We started to yell, as loud as we could, to try and find Jasper. How could we have lost him?" continued Rupert. "He had been there a minute ago but had disappeared when the torch light failed. We thought he must be nearby, but knew he would answer our calls if he was."

"I held on tightly to the piece of string in my hand that would lead us out of the mine," continued Sam. "It was an old worn-out piece of string I had been carefully unwinding as we entered the mine, it would be our way out of the nightmare. While Rupert and Jasper had been arguing about who should be the leader, I had quickly taken the opportunity to fasten the string to a post at the entrance. But we were unable to leave without Jasper; we couldn't abandon him there."

"I felt a hand slip into mine. I didn't know if it was Rupert's or Sam's, I was relieved to have contact with someone… anyone," Jasper said, dismally. "The hand felt cold and clammy, strangely misshapen with a vicelike grip. Fear can make people overreact, and I rationalized that whoever was holding my hand must be terrified, so I didn't cry out even though my hand was being crushed. With the deafening noise of the boulders scraping along the seabed I found it difficult to hear my friend, but reasoned he was too frightened to talk. I took a few deep breaths and tried to calm myself saying that I was sure we had been facing right, when my torch gave way, so if we turned left, we should be heading back towards the entrance. I reasoned with myself that if we managed to exit the mine, we could seek help to find our missing friend. I knew we would be in dire straits for entering the mine, but we could face the consequences after the rescue had been completed.

"I started to lead the way out but soon realised the ground had remained level for too long, by that time I should have reached the steep incline that led out of the mine. Maybe time had slowed down as it often does when you're in a bad situation, and it was more than bad, it was horrendous.

"Puzzlingly, I heard a racket on the other side of the walls, outside the mine, it stopped me in my tracks. It was a rumbling and moving sensation in the sea, different from the boulder turbulence, more rhythmical and flowing rather than harsh and crashing. Also, I could hear a deep groaning and rasping sound as if something enormous was trying to draw breath after strenuous exercise. Curiosity got the better of me, my fear seemed to drain away. I knew some creature was in distress and needed my help, I would do all that I was capable of to assist. Grabbing my torch by my teeth — I wasn't going to lose it even if it didn't work — I put my free hand flat on the wall nearest to the noise. I immediately felt its presence. It was swimming backwards and forwards, concentrating on one place as if it was trying to complete a task. It came to me that perhaps it was trying to stop the sea water entering the mine or maybe stop something seeping out of the mine. The concept seemed to drift into my mind, and I knew it was true.

"As it became aware of my proximity, the creature slowed down, virtually stopped. I heard the steady thud of its enormous heart sending shock waves across the water, through the seabed, old mine timbers and concrete walls, finding its destination — my hands. The vibration of its heart rhythm spreading across my body had a steadying effect on me, leading me to believe our heartbeats were trying to match each other; we were synchronising. A clear thought emerged, indicating we had some history, some shared ancient history; we knew each other from eons past. The whole atmosphere changed, from noisy frenzied activity to a quiet, peaceful state. I tentatively moved my hand across the wall and began to get an impression of its size. It was huge. From head to tail it was an unimaginable size and the strength it possessed was immeasurable. If this creature had any intention of harming me, it could tear the mine down as easily as a knife cuts through butter. I was certain the creature was aware of my dilemma. Perhaps it was trying to help me to find my way out. Then it was gone, as if it had some important job to complete and was unable to stay; it had to continue with its task. Startlingly, the mine became eerily quiet."

"The Lee family has always had an understanding with animals," mused Old Ben.

"Magical quality," added someone from the back of the room.

Jasper took a deep breath and continued, "Knowing my friend would be able to hear me, now that the deafening noise had died down, I told Sam or Rupert, that I had sensed something on the other side of the wall but didn't get any reply. I didn't repeat myself, thinking they were terrified. I understood that this wasn't the time or place to talk about what I'd just experienced. The priority was to get out of the mine.

"I said we were probably going the wrong way; we should backtrack, find another route. My suggestion was met with silence, so I tried again in a reassuring voice. I said that it might take a long time to find our way out, but we would do it, we just needed to stay positive, keep trying. The hand tightened its grip notch by notch. I couldn't help but cry out in pain. Suddenly the hand let go of me and tried to grab my torch, but I was too quick and tore the hand away from it. I was sure that it was Rupert, trying to snatch my torch again. To my horror the hand ripped away from its wrist, and I was left holding it; limp and lifeless. I screamed in terror. What was happening? The torch crashed to the ground with a shattering sound. As it hit the floor the light made a connection and flickered back on. I stared at the bloody stump where the jagged bones and foul flesh hung loose. I stared at the empty space where the arm should be.

"Feeling sick and dizzy I fell against the wall and screamed. Scuttling away from me into the shadows was a small, grotesque, manlike creature. He turned around menacingly, fixing me with a cold stare, laughing hysterically and holding up his arm that was dripping with blood. He snarled at me showing hundreds of rotten, pointed teeth that looked as sharp as razors. Throwing the hand onto the floor I tried to back away from him, but my legs were like jelly, they wouldn't move. I was trapped. He walked over to the hand, picked it up and held it to his arm… unbelievably they re-joined!

"I knew it was a piskie and kept my eyes fixed on him, trying to rationalise that it was a trick, smoke and mirrors but that didn't quell my fear. I knew his intention. He meant to harm me. I was petrified. He was treacherous and evil, not like his contemporaries who were mischievous and full of trickery. Trying to confuse me by leading me into the depths of the mine, his purpose was for me to become lost forever. He would take pleasure from frightening and tormenting me in the eternal darkness of the abandoned mine. I would become his plaything, a distraction from his boredom. That's when I heard Sam and Rupert calling for me. They must had seen my torch light and came running towards me. The piskie gave me one last withering look and in a hissing voice ridiculed my fear. He vanished into the shadowy nooks and crannies of the dark, damp walls immediately before Sam reached my side, but I knew Sam had seen him.

"Sam quietened me, he held me until I stopped shaking. He told me we were going to get out of that dreadful place. I was gabbling hysterically about piskies and sea creatures. Sam said to try not to think about anything, just follow him out of the mine, ignore the mischievous tricks piskies use to frighten and confuse people. At that moment we were plunged back into darkness again, my torch had finally stopped working, but Rupert and Sam kept their composure, and we started to stumble out of the deep, damp crypt by following that thin piece of string. I was so jittery I insisted on walking in the middle."

"We recognised we were heading in the right direction as we reached the steep incline," Rupert continued. "At first, I wasn't convinced Jasper had seen the piskie or that he had made a connection with the sea creature, but I kept my opinion to myself. Sorry Jasper, it's the first time I've admitted that."

"That's understandable, emotions were running pretty high. I realise it was hard to believe."

"I was leading my friends slowly up the incline, trailing one hand on the wall, so I wouldn't walk into it," Sam sighed. "We were like the three blind mice, and I knew that the farmer's wife was hot on our heels with her carving knife. I tried not to think about the string being old and worn — it could break at any time. If it broke, we would lose our lifeline. I felt a tugging sensation on the top of my sneakers. I panicked, not knowing what it was. Shaking my legs, to rid myself of whatever was there I realised, too late, my shoelaces had been tied together. For one hopeful moment I imagined I wouldn't fall. I very nearly gained my balance, but a sharp blow to the back of my legs accompanied by harsh cackling laughter sent me tumbling to the ground in a heap. I banged my head on the floor, and my tongue felt the rough edge of a chipped tooth. Rupert and Jasper stopped in their tracks, they quickly bent down to help me. Fighting back tears I said I was fine. A foul putrid breath was blasted into my face, like slimy, rotting flowers on a neglected grave."

"You won't be leaving this place boys!" continued Rupert, in a voice imitating the malevolent piskie. "In my nightmares I still hear his menacing voice. From somewhere deep in the confines of the mine, somewhere no one wanted to be, someone or something was threatening us. I realised it must be the piskie. Sam shouted that we shouldn't listen to him, he was trying to confuse us, and we were scarcely minutes from the entrance where we would be safe."

"Still holding the string in my hand, I knew we had to remain focused and follow its lead. I sat up and slipped off my sneakers. As I pulled on the string there was no resistance, it had snapped," Sam added dismally. "I heard the hysterical laughter of the piskie, who was clearly enjoying our fear and panic. I wasn't going to let him win. I wasn't going to remain lost in the mine. I wasn't going to die there. Pulling myself up, I put my hand on the wall and continued to lead my friends out of the nightmare. As we burst from the mine the Cornish air had never smelled so sweet. Collapsing onto the headland, we started laughing uncontrollably. At the time it seemed a totally inappropriate response, but years later I realised it was because we were in shock. We couldn't believe we had woken up from the nightmare."

"Of course, we talked about it when we were sitting on Botack Headland," Rupert said, "but we decided to stay quiet, keep it to ourselves. Apart from being in trouble for entering the mine, who was going to believe the story about a gigantic sea creature, a piskie and a fracture in the concrete wall? We had to think of an excuse for Sam's injuries, as his face looked a bit of a mess, and a part of his front tooth was missing! We also had to think of a story for Sam's missing sneakers — they had been left in the mine."

Jasper laughed, saying, "We decided to say we had

been playing football on the beach, and Sam had fallen onto a rock — it would account for the chipped tooth."

"We embellished the story saying that we had been playing football barefoot when my sneakers had been swept away by a rogue wave," Sam added.

"Have you heard of an imaginarium, boys?" queried Megan Genn. "It's a place where your imagination runs free and, in your case, wild. It's nothing more than three boys scaring the pants off each other!"

Some members of the assembly agreed with her outburst, but others looked acutely uncomfortable, including Eleanor and Anna.

"That might be your opinion, Megan," interrupted Edith, aiming at halting any more negative comments. "We are here to listen to everyone's ideas and suggestions, however outlandish." Edith was about to continue when she heard Eleanor speaking very quietly, almost to herself. "What did you say Eleanor? You can express yourself here. No one will judge you." Edith glared at Megan who folded her arms and shook he head.

"He called your name," Eleanor stated.

"How did you know? I've never told anyone that!" declared Jasper.

"The piskie knew your name, he said Jasper," continued Eleanor. "I heard you scream and knew you were terrified. I was on the beach at Porthenby, enjoying the day checking on the rock pools, when I felt your terror. It caused me to struggle with my breathing. It barely lasted a moment, but in that time I saw the mine and realised you were trapped inside. The piskie has been exiled there by his tribe, they realised he was too dangerous to be allowed to wander free above ground. He must remain there until he is contrite, where he is unable to do harm to any living creature. Entombed in the concrete crypt. I knew it was going to be difficult for me to get help to you, as no one would believe me. I feared ridicule, which has followed me all my life, but I had to try and persuade someone, anyone, that you boys were lost in the old undersea tin mine; in grave danger. The piskie was angry, he wanted to harm you all, but he particularly hated you Jasper because of the connection you made with the Dragon. He had been trying to make that connection for years.

"I rushed off the beach and decided I would go to Phoebe's cottage at Sennen Cove. She would listen. Anna would take me there in her car. First, she would listen, then offer her reasonable explanation of what I had experienced on the beach. Probably to convince herself as well as me, but we didn't have time to stand and talk — the three of you were in grave danger. I refused to listen to her, and seeing how distraught I was she quickly got her car out of the garage. It was then that I saw you boys walking past my cottage, making your way home, deep in conversation. I was extremely relieved to see you. Anna, sensing the ease in my agitated state led me back into our cottage. She said everything was fine, I should get some rest."

The silence was broken by Jasper going over to Eleanor and hugging her. "Thank you, Eleanor."

"I think we may have found an answer to our question here. Maybe the fracture in the tin mine has widened, maybe the old tanks full of poisonous gas are leaking into the sea," suggested Ben.

"Could be earth tremors over the decades that have weakened the reinforced walls. And the tanks, stored underground in the damp, salty mine — they could have corroded. Who knows how long they are able to restrain their deadly content? Stands to reason they aren't going to last forever," added Harry.

"The piskie could have caused the problem with the wall. We've all heard how evil he is," whispered Eleanor.

"Or it could be fanciful ideas from young boys that over the years have grown malignantly into a monster of a story!" Megan declared.

"All good valid points," Edith said summing up the multiple contributions, which came flying from all directions of the room. "What we need to do now is take action. We need to check out this tin mine, see if there's a problem there, if there is then we need to deal with it. If not, then we have to keep searching for answers. Whatever is causing the damage to life, on our land, sea and air, needs to be put right."

Suddenly the kitchen door burst open, banging against the wall, startling everyone. Molly Lee strode into the room looking distressed. Jasper and Jack immediately went over to her and held her tightly; something was drastically wrong.

Baa, Baa, Black Sheep

Molly had not attended the meeting, she had decided to stay at home stating that someone needed to be around to supervise the lambing, it was a crucial time of the year. Over the years, she had found that it was beneficial for her to be around when the new lambs were born, giving comfort and a feeling of wellbeing to the ewes. They felt safe in her presence, which helped the birthing process. Although their sheep were strong healthy stock, the Lee family never left anything to chance; they were always on call for their animals' welfare.

During the year lots of discussions had been held in the family concerning the black sheep in their flock whose fleeces were traditionally less sought after than their contemporary white fleeces. The black lambs only popped up occasionally and were a talking point in and around the area. When one was born, passers-by would point it out in the fields and marvel at the stark difference. Children would chant the old nursery rhyme as they passed the lamb on their way to school, giggling and laughing at its sooty presence gambolling around amongst the flurry of snow-white lambs.

Jack had suggested they try to breed a few more black lambs, as the fashion industry seemed to be taking an interest in this rare wool. He noticed the black fleece was much softer to the touch and was sure it would produce a more comfortable silky yarn with a beautiful drape: he had identified a new market. Jasper and Molly agreed with his idea which was going to be difficult to achieve, but the Lee family always liked to rise to a challenge. They were pleased their son was taking an interest in the family business.

Jasper, together with his son, had carefully and methodically selected their prospective sheep, with the hope that their offspring would be endowed with the black fleece. The gene for this unusual fleece is recessive, and Jack had spent many hours trawling through the history of their breeding stock to identify which ewes and rams would increase the odds of the black fleece being present in the next generation. It was gambling odds, and Jack always loved games of chance. After identifying around twenty prospective sheep, Jasper helped his son with the final decision, ten healthy, robust ewes and Cyril, their new ram — who they suspected carried the recessive gene. Fashion-fleece, the project had been named, and it would hopefully be another profitable opening for their business.

"Jasper, you need to come home," Molly sobbed. "Our ten fashion-fleece ewes have all given birth. The lambs are dead, they didn't even draw breath."

Jasper looked shocked. How could this be? He had examined all ten ewes this morning and had felt the new energetic life surging through them. None of them were first time lambers, all of them were fit and healthy; there had been nothing to worry about. After checking them over he had led them into the sea-facing field with its lush grass as a special treat for them. The grass, which was full of minerals and natural goodness from its proximity to the sea, would be beneficial for the ewes, soothing them in preparation for lambing. Storm clouds swiftly flew through his mind. Perhaps something from the sea had poisoned the grass in the field. Or maybe they had dabbled too much with nature. Rare things were meant to be rare, or they would lose their value. "Come on Molly, let's go home, we'll see what's happened." Jasper grabbed his coat and led Molly out of the kitchen.

Jack made his way back to Chesten, "I have to go and help." Leaning down he kissed her on her cheek before racing through the door after his parents.

It seemed to Edith that a call to action was needed, the situation was getting worse with each passing day. These incidents could be coincidental or maybe related, things needed checking out. The meeting broke up shortly afterwards, with an agreement that investigations would begin immediately on the old undersea tin mine. A working party would be assembled, headed by Rupert who would organise the project.

You Can Go Too

Phoebe took a sip of her tea, and looked around the room at all the people she held closest to her heart. Her family was trying to relax after the evening's eventful meeting. Sam and Edith were sitting together on the sofa, his arm draped protectively over her shoulder. Her granddaughters were sitting at her feet, so different in looks and personality, but both strongly linked by their close sibling bond. Phoebe knew she was blessed to have such a loving family. The firelight cast warm welcoming light onto the scene, gradually thawing the atmosphere which had frosted over during the assembly. Cove Cottage was working its magic, erasing any anxiety.

"Can you finish your story, nan? Tamara asked pleadingly.

"How did you get there? How did you manage to enter the cave?" asked Chesten, leading Phoebe back into her story.

She cast her mind back to the morning after Tom's first sighting of the Dragon, when they had decided to take action and help her. It had been a reckless decision, fraught with danger, but they had both been young and full of a sense of adventure; anything was possible.

"In the early hours of the morning, before breakfast, your grandad announced he would be taking the boat to Mermaid Cave, I could go too. He understood my anxiety about the sea and said he was capable of checking on the

Dragon himself if the journey into the cave was going to be too stressful for me. But your grandad knew I would be unable to let him go alone… I needed to see the Dragon myself.

“He’d scrutinised the tide times, sea levels, weather and moon phases saying it was a perfect time to enter the cave. Being adventurous and thirsty for knowledge of all the sea caves around the coast, your grandad had sailed into Mermaid Cave on a few occasions. It was dangerous, but he was an excellent sailor and wouldn’t take any unnecessary risks. Knowing there was a high ledge of rock, which ran along the back of the cave, he said we would climb up there and wait for the Dragon to appear — the tides were low for the next few days so the sea wouldn’t reach that level; we would be safe. We would need to take food and water because we would be unable to leave until the tide was about to turn, before that time the current would be too strong to fight against. We aimed to set off at six o’clock, the light would be fading, but there would be a full moon that night and we could take waterproof flashlights.

“During the afternoon I went to see my mum, to let her know where I would be going. Your grandad said not to worry people, but I knew it was the right thing to do. After all, if something unexpected did happen, how would anyone find us if they didn’t know where to look? Mum was at work tending to an old sick dog. She had such a kind way with the animals she treated, her caring touch was as effective as the medication she gave her furry patients. Small kind deeds can have a huge impact, she would often say to me. I’m sure she was right. By spending time at her surgery, when I was a young girl, I learnt a great deal about animals. I even considered following in her footsteps by becoming a veterinary surgeon, but I chose a different route.

"Mum was distraught when she heard of our plan and tried to persuade me against the journey into Mermaid Cave. She stated the Dragon didn't need my help but she hadn't seen her. I was sure I was right.

"Nan, you're contradicting yourself," interrupted Tamara, "you said the Dragon would always sort things out herself. Leave well alone."

Chesten searched her grandmother's face and body language. How was she going to get out of this one? Do as I say not as I do. Surprisingly, she didn't flinch.

"I know what I said Tamara, but remember we were young and invincible, or so we thought. We wanted to set matters right. Also remember I was going into the cave with your grandad, the best sailor in the world!"

Tamara sighed. Chesten noted her sister wasn't satisfied with their nan's reasoning, but it would have to do if they wanted her to continue with the story.

"All of my mum's protestations fell on deaf ears. She knew how stubborn I could be; I was going with your grandad. Pressing a large jar of her latest development into my hands she quickly ran through the instructions for its use. It was an ointment, designed to alleviate severe skin conditions in cattle. Mum had spent many hours researching various medications and their effectiveness and had started to produce her own. I'm reminded of my mum every time I see Edith developing new glazes; both of them trailblazers! Such imagination and tenacity. At that point the ointment hadn't been approved for use, it needed to go through a trial period and be tested on specific groups of cattle. She was very careful to follow the strict guidelines that controlled the designing of new drugs, so it was a gesture of hope when she passed the ointment over to me. If she couldn't stop me from going, maybe her salve would help the Dragon. Neither of us knew if it would work or not, but it was worth a try. What else could we do?”

Tamara shook her head at the recklessness of her nan’s decision. Chesten wondered what she would do if she was ever in the same position as her nan had been. She knew the answer even before she had formulated the question — she would help the Dragon.

The Dragon's Lair

Phoebe noted the dismissive shake of Tamara's head, and knew her granddaughter was about to interrupt her again with one of her abrasive remarks. She quickly picked up the narrative, preventing any disruption of her story. One of her journalist tricks. "We boarded our boat, *Pheebz,* just after six o'clock that evening. The sun was low in the sky, even so we would have enough light to make our way into the cave. I was apprehensive, although part of me loved the idea of being alone on the sea with your grandad, I wasn't at home on the boat. The constantly churning sea and the tiny boat pitched against the vast ocean unsettled me, but this was a journey I had to make if I intended to help the Dragon. On the open sea I always felt my grasp of control was torn away from me," Phoebe admitted.

"As the opening to the cave appeared, I wondered how on earth we would gain entry; it was too small. It grew larger as we approached but still seemed a tight fit. I crossed my fingers, hoping we would be able to steer through. Your grandad's timing was impeccable, and the tide speedily pushed the boat into the tumultuous waters of the cave. He had warned me about this part of the journey, so I tried to relax by putting my faith in his seafaring capabilities. Expertly manoeuvring the boat to the back of the cave, *Pheebz* hit the wall with an almighty bump that brought us to a sudden halt. As agile as a cat he jumped off the boat and landed onto a large rock jutting out from the wall of the cave. He quickly tied the boat and helped me to get off, knowing I would feel more comfortable as soon as my feet felt the security of the solid rock.

"Surprisingly, from such a small entrance, the cave opened up into a large circular area with steep, jagged, granite walls leading up to a high roof. It reminded me of an old cathedral, tall and imposing with the ocean swirling around like a congregation searching for their seats. I looked up and saw the ledge your grandad had told me about, but it didn't look high enough to me. I had a vision of the sea rushing in and sweeping us away into the cold Atlantic Ocean. I shook my head and realised that couldn't happen — your grandad knew the sea.

"As we climbed the narrow, slippery path towards the ledge, it occurred to me we had entered the Dragon's lair. How would this wild, untamed creature respond to such an intrusion? I had seen animals that were frightened or felt threatened, in my mother's veterinary practice. They would often act out of nature, sometimes fearful and withdrawn, at other times threatening and aggressive. It took mum quite a while to gain their trust before she was able to tend to their needs. But we wouldn't have that time. If the Dragon considered us a threat, how was she going to respond? I didn't want to think about it."

Edith moved position on the settee, leaning forwards, enabling her to gather all the details of her mother's description of the Dragon's lair. She didn't want to miss any part of it. As a child she had begged for this episode of the story to be told, over and over, it was her favourite part. With each retelling, Edith would glean more information from the description, there was always something new added to the story, some hidden memory that made itself known. It almost felt as if the memory had become her own.

Phoebe noticed her daughter's interest and smiled to herself as she continued with her story, "On reaching the ledge, it was obvious that it was the place where the Dragon rested. Dried seaweed was strewn along the whole length of the rocky spur which served as bedding for the Dragon. In one corner, old, discarded fish bones were present, suggesting she ate there. I hoped we wouldn't end up in the same place. On the opposite corner was the opening of the blowing hole, the portal which led to its sea facing outlet. The area was packed with soft, padded down seaweed. We surmised that it must have been where the Dragon rested to release her magic breath that would explode out of the blowing hole and dissipate throughout Porthenby; to help maintain the status quo.

"After we had examined her lair, your grandad secured the boat, tethering the rope with enough slack to allow for the rising flood tide. In the light of the situation we had placed ourselves in he was remarkably placid, which served to ease any last vestiges of anxiety in me. We waited there, unsure what would happen next, maybe nothing. If that was so, we would pass the time enjoying the solitude of our surroundings, until the tide turned. Then we would make our way home through the night sky. We chatted about moving to the south coast, as the disaster hadn't reached there, so your grandad could continue fishing. For me, the lure of a milder sea was tempting. I would be more relaxed when your grandad was out on the open sea, believing he would be safer. The north coast was in our blood but, at times, the sea and weather were totally unpredictable and dangerous. I loved your grandad with all my heart, so I was willing to make the move, for his safety. I knew it would tear your grandad apart leaving the north coast, he loved every aspect of the ocean, but if he couldn't fish there we would have to move," Phoebe sighed, the memory of the evening seemed fresh and young, but it had been a long time ago.

"As the light was starting to fade I reached for my torch, but your grandad put his hand over mine as if to say not yet. He nodded towards the entrance where the ocean was rushing in and the setting sun was casting deep long shadows along the walls. I was startled by a huge wave crashing against the sides of the cave, spilling water and foam along their shadowy length. Silhouetted against the westerly sun's dying rays, we saw the Dragon make her entrance through the mouth of the cave. She was a wreck of a sight: as weak as a kitten, scales sloughing off her body, exposing skin rubbed raw by the oil and chemicals she had been fighting. We were shocked to see her in such a state. Despite her size and might she had become a fragile thing. I wasn't afraid of her. I could tell by the way she presented herself she meant no harm. I was adept at recognising fear, aggression and trust in animals."

"I know what you mean nan, I can tell if an animal is in pain or if it's distressed. If it intends to harm me or not."

"You've spent a lot of time working with large animals, Chesten, so you're able to read their body language," Sam said. "Sometimes I think you are more attuned to the cows' behaviour and manner than me!"

Tamara scowled at her sister as a warning to stay quiet, let nan tell her story.

Phoebe picked up her thread, "Your grandad held me close while we watched mesmerised as the Dragon swam slowly towards the back of the cave, towards us. Struggling to get out of the water and climb up the rocky incline, my heart went out to her. She was a shadow of her former self. As she trudged up her well-worn path the unusual way she moved, resting on her right legs and dragging her left side, suggested she was in pain. Her once prominent spikes, which ran the full length of her body from head to tail, were drooping and peculiarly translucent. Her spirit was confined, deep within her body and was unable to shine through the dull, opaque eyes. Her short, rasping breath prevented the massive lungs from inflating, causing her body to become starved of lifesaving oxygen. What could we possibly do to help this creature? As she rested, near the onset of the blowing hole, the Dragon desperately tried to breathe her magic through the portal. She needed to perform her part of the jigsaw; fulfil her role. She was failing. A dying creature trying to save her home. It was her duty, she would continue with her role until the day she died, like a Celtic queen fighting an invading army.

"With your grandad by my side I wasn't afraid and sat down next to her, stroking her head; it was an instinctive act. Her skin felt surprisingly soft and pliable. I could feel the muscle under my hand, it was wasting away. She nudged me with her long snout as if to thank me for my kind touch and concern. I felt tears streaming down my cheeks and watched as they landed on her head rolling down her long serpent-like neck, onto her body. I wondered how tears could travel so far. It wasn't possible. Your grandad passed the ointment to me, encouraging me to try it. I wasn't sure. Not wanting to make matters worse and possibly cause her more pain I was unwilling to use it. The ointment hadn't been tested, it may cause more damage, but what other option did I have? Your grandad carefully unscrewed the lid and handed it to me. He was certain the Dragon trusted me and that I could help her — just believe it, he said.

"Reluctantly, I took a small amount into the palm of

my hand and gently massaged her head. I was surprised that such a small amount covered the whole of her head and snout. Immediately the skin there took on a lustrous glow, like an open oyster shell displaying iridescent colours. As she responded to the treatment, her spirit broke through the barrier of pain, and her eyes became saturated with deep pools of ocean blue. She turned her head to look at me, and I started to fall into the depths of her soul. It was a peculiar sensation, drowning in the depths of the blue, I wanted to stay there forever. Her age gradually started to reveal itself to me. Like counting the growth rings of an ancient tree, I slowly began to perceive her immeasurable time upon this earth, unlike our fleeting path. I also sensed a shared past. A time when all living organisms existed side by side, in harmony with nature. A time when dragons were an accepted part of the world, not forced to seek the safety of myth or legend. Reluctantly I dragged myself back from that beautiful place, I had a job to complete. Amazingly I managed to cover every part of her body with the ointment. It took hours to accomplish. I didn't stop for one moment. As the ointment emptied from the jar, the task was concluded. Her gratitude and trust had grown during the hours we had spent together. I'm certain that with the aid of the ointment and your grandad by her side talking gently and soothingly, she was rested, repaired and revitalised. Her breathing was becoming stronger, more regular, and the blowing hole was starting to work again. Her muscles were becoming more powerful, enabling her to stand and walk perfectly balanced. Once again, her pliant scales fully covered her enormous body, displaying her full magnificence. My Dragon."

Chesten sighed and reached for Tamara's hand as they both pictured the Dragon, repaired — saved by their nan and grandad!

"We hadn't noticed the hours passing and the tide turning, but the Dragon had. As the tide was about to turn the Dragon stood up tall and proud, queen of the seas again. She turned to look at us and paused, as if she wanted to stay but was unable to. Some far away duty was calling, the Dragon needed to attend to it. Turning seawards she slipped into the water which by this time had reached a metre or so below the high ledge. With a few twists of her body, she swam out of the cave, into the night ocean. The moonlight danced upon her now prominent spines, revealing a luminous mountain range slicing through the water as she made her way out to sea, towards the horizon. We wondered where she was going.

"I was startled to see how high the sea had risen. The entrance to the cave was virtually obscured by water, with an ever-decreasing small gap between ocean and the top of the cave, our exit. Your grandad said we would be able to negotiate the passage, but we couldn't delay until the ebb tide grew stronger and the water level dropped because strong currents and eddies would manifest, making our departure impossible."

"How did you get out of Mermaid Cave?" demanded Tamara. "Everyone knows it's virtually impossible."

Chesten noticed the irritation in her sister's tone. Nan would have some explaining to do.

"I've heard that it's easier to get into the cave than out," said Chesten.

"Yes girls, you are both right, but remember your grandad was an excellent sailor, and although it was difficult, we managed it. I wouldn't be here to tell the tale if not. I wouldn't have entered the cave with anyone but your grandad, and no one else should ever attempt it." Phoebe looked directly at Chesten and Tamara in order to accentuate the point. She didn't want her granddaughters to go through the same experience she had. Looking back, they had been lucky to survive the whole ordeal.

Edith loved to hear stories about her father. Chesten had been barely twelve years old and Tamara eleven when he had been cruelly snatched away from them in a horrific traffic accident. She missed her father every day, and it hurt to think her children had been denied the love of a caring grandfather.

"It was tricky, I must admit," continued Phoebe shaking her head. "As we approached the mouth of the cave, the boat was remarkably steady in the water, the ocean seemed to be having a rest before she resumed her crazy jiggling around. I was frozen to the spot, extremely anxious, holding my breath. Your grandad laughed at me, telling me to breathe and relax, to enjoy the ride. As he steered through the mouth, I reached up and actually touched the top of the opening! Tiny sharp edges of rock moved along my hand, like canine teeth readying themselves for a feast. It was scary — if the tide had been rougher, we would have been stuck in the cave; there wasn't any other way out. We both heaved a sigh of relief when we reached the open sea. I hadn't realised your grandad had been worried. I'd been sure he had it all under control, but I understood at that moment how dangerous the situation had been. We were both young and silly, like your father and his friends daring each other to go into the mine — it was a risk we shouldn't have taken.

"It was on that day that I realised I loved your grandad more than I ever imagined was possible. He had taken me into the cave to save the Dragon. My Dragon. The full moon had risen and the sky was clear, making it bright enough to steer *Pheebz* back home safely. Tom shouted for me to look starboard. That's when I saw her. My beautiful, magnificent creature. She was lying in the ocean, transforming herself into a massive sea break. Twisting and turning her body to deflect the brunt of the waves, which were being targeted at Mermaid Cave. The Dragon had saved us from a watery grave. I'm sure of it."

Time To Go Home

Chesten and Tamara quietly mulled over the events of the story, feeling a little resentful. They couldn't believe someone had sailed into Mermaid Cave and back out… and lived to tell the tale. What made it even more incredulous was that the adventurers had been their nan and grandad! It had quickened their imagination and sense of adventure, despite their nan's warning. Chesten thought it was a tad unfair that nan had disregarded her own mother's advice and pleas and had recklessly gone ahead with her escapade, then warned them not to do anything like it themselves. Do as I say not as I do. The old saying edged its way into her mind and niggled her.

"Enough story telling for tonight, it's getting late. Mum, why not stay here? I can make a bed up for you. It's silly going home at this time," Edith beseeched. "Stay for the night, you can go home first thing in the morning."

"Nonsense, its only 11 o'clock with a beautiful full moon to guide me home. I'll ring as soon as I get in, so don't worry." Not allowing the past to make her life smaller, Phoebe picked up her car keys. She was more than capable of driving herself home — safely.

Locking the kitchen door after her mother left, Edith turned to Sam, and demanded an answer to the question she had been waiting all night to ask, "Why didn't you tell me the truth about how you chipped your tooth?" The house was quiet, the girls were in bed, and now she had Sam's undivided attention. He had some explaining to do. How could he have lied to her all these years?

Sam pondered for a while, worrying away at his chipped tooth with his tongue. "It was all a long time ago, after that eventful day we didn't mention it again… until tonight. That day gradually faded from my memory, and I didn't want to relive any part of it. I've told the story of my chipped tooth being a football accident so many times that it gradually became a truth for me. Tonight, during the meeting, something clicked in my brain and the floodgates opened. All the details of that horrific day started to sweep through me. It struck me, like a bolt of lightning, that maybe the undersea tin mine could be the source of our problems. When the three of us started to add our different parts to the story, making it a whole, it was like solving a puzzle. I realised what actually happened. I didn't think I had lied to you Edith, but I understand now that I have… and I'm sorry."

Edith, knowing Sam was contrite, held his hand and said it was fine she understood. She didn't intend adding to his troubled state but had needed to clear the air; they had always been honest with each other. Drawing Sam into her arms she realised he was crying. It would be alright she said, gently rocking him. Everything would work out fine.

Tamara had been exhausted after the day's events, falling asleep as soon as her head touched the pillow. Unlike her sister, who was unable to summon sleep as she tossed and turned, thoughts flitting in and out of her mind like busy bees searching for nectar. Memories of her grandad brought a sense of peace and tranquillity to her tired mind, but they were tinged with the pain of sadness and loss. Trying unsuccessfully to conjure up an image of him, Chesten screwed up her eyes and concentrated. A picture started forming, but it was blurred and frayed around the edges. She desperately wanted to see that face again. Remembering events and outings in more detail than his features, she sighed with annoyance. Her sister was able to recall his bone structure and facial details with such precision, it amazed Chesten. Her own memories were hiding away, too deep inside her, resisting her coaxing manner. They were disjointed, refusing to make a whole picture. Her grandmother's stories added depth to these shy, elusive recollections, which drew more on his personality and traits rather than his appearance. Nevertheless, they built up a rounded, realistic person, but Chesten longed to bring to life that kind, weathered face.

Calling to mind his bright red hair, she felt a warmth settle over her. Everyone said Tom's hair colour was a gift to Chesten. She touched her face where the tough whiskers would scratch her cheeks when he kissed her — hoping to feel the faint scratches there. They had disappeared long ago. She longed to hear the cheery voice that had sung sea shanties to her at bed time, creating images of life on the open sea. They had lulled her into salty dreams where she swam through mermaids' caves and found hidden treasures in the sunken remains of a Tudor boat. She craved the exhilaration of the strong arms lifting her high into the air, spinning her around, making her laugh. And where was the familiar warmth of the sunshine and smell of the sea that followed him everywhere? She couldn't clearly picture his face: even photos didn't clarify the memory. But she had more, she had the essence of him. Sleep crept over the threshold, swaddling her in its comforting embrace. With her grandad as her guardian.

A Boat Is Named

Phoebe enjoyed the solitude of driving at night, the daytime traffic had gone to sleep and the winding country roads were too familiar to pose a problem. The moon was full and bright, standing high in the clear sky, presenting an enticing softly illumined path that would lead her home. It was a peaceful time of the day to reminisce. The meeting tonight and the telling of her story had tired her, allowing her mind to uncharacteristically wander wherever it chose. Skipping over youthful adventures, past playmates, times at school and helping her mum at the vet's practice, her mind settled on its favourite memory... Tom. Her line of thought kept nudging its way towards the accident, but Phoebe fought against it. It persevered and because she was fatigued, the floodgates slowly began to open, allowing it to trickle in. She resented its intrusion and tried to cling onto the good recollections. She didn't need the pain and anguish of the horrendous memories, but at times was unable to shake free of them.

As the car headed home, Phoebe began to recall Tom's dream of building his fishing fleet. She had been supportive and proud when he began to upgrade his fishing boats. He had acquired quite a few upgrades since their first purchase, *Pheebz*, and the fishing was plentiful. He still kept the small fishing boat, perhaps it was sentimentality or because he presumed that he wouldn't be able to get a good price for her. Or maybe because he knew that their granddaughter Chesten would never forgive him if he sold her.

Years ago, when they were first married, Tom had spent days preparing and painting the boat in a beautiful sea blue shade, Phoebe's favourite colour, and left the boat locked up for the night in a secured boatyard. A sign writer was due to join him to scribe the boat's name — *Phoebe* on the stern and both sides of the bow. This was aimed at being a surprise for his wife and he knew she would be pleased. Tom had chosen a deep black paint, outlined in gold which he knew would contrast perfectly with the boat's sea blue colour.

When he met up with the sign writer, early the next morning, he had eagerly opened up the boatyard and made his way towards the boat. To his amazement and confusion, the boat had been named *Pheebz*, perfectly italicized in black paint and outlined in gold. It looked good, more than good, it was excellent. He wondered who on earth had managed to get into the boatyard — he had the sole key to the place. Furthermore, why would someone do this? Looking puzzled, the sign writer turned to him for an explanation. Tom had shrugged his shoulders, offering the only explanation he could, stating it must have been the piskies! Both Tom and she had laughed until their sides ached at his explanation. Tom said the piskies were annoyed they hadn't managed to get an angry response from him. They loved ranters and ravers because it made their pranks all the more enjoyable. He said the piskies had slouched away into the dark nooks and crannies of the building, but he noticed one piskie, maybe an elder, sitting in the rafters surveying the actions as they unfolded. He had waved at the piskie and laughed.

Phoebe had loved the boat's name, she even said that

she preferred it. She revelled in Tom's romantic nature; it made her feel loved. On days when he knew the fishing wouldn't be worthwhile he would suggest they took the boat out on a pleasure cruise. Just me and you on the open sea, he would say pleadingly. She usually agreed to the outings, feeling the need to show the young and adventurous side of her nature to her new husband, but she was always cautious of the sea; preferring her feet to be on dry land. Tom would appear concerned at her agitation when she was aboard *Pheebz* and would try to calm her by pointing out the beauty of their surroundings. She was unable to respond in any favourable manner, and as they skimmed through the ocean her anxiety would spread through the boat like soft butter on warm bread. The wooden hull soaked up her fear, causing the boat to slow in her reaction to Tom's skippering. Tom often said that when he fished alone with *Pheebz,* the experience was beneficial to both parties. The boat relished being out on the open sea and responded to his attentiveness by ensuring he was safe, even when they plunged through massive waves with steadfast bravery and determination.

Although she had loved to hear about his seafaring adventures it saddened her to think she had been unable to be part of the experiences. She knew that Tom had hoped one day her fears would be dispelled, like rolling dark thunder clouds giving way to brilliant sunshine, but it didn't happen. If they ever encountered even the smallest change in the weather, which would cause the boat to roll with the waves, he would witness her panic grow. Tom had been so understanding and realised she would never conquer her deep-rooted fear of the sea, so he had changed tactics and began to encourage land-based pastimes, such as picnics on Porthenby Island. Tom had repeatedly said he loved her and could change his ways; he didn't expect her to alter. He stated they could picnic near the sea but not on it, which would make them both happy. When their daughter was born, Tom said life couldn't get any better. Tentatively he had asked if she liked the name Anahita, meaning water or river goddess. They could shorten it to Anna for everyday use, he suggested. But she had been adamant on the name Edith, saying they had been blessed with the arrival of a baby girl. Tom knew she wouldn't encourage their daughter to develop a love of the sea. He understood her need to protect their child. As the years passed, they had settled into a comfortable routine, and he constantly told her how much he loved her — as much as the day they were married. He had been an old romantic at heart.

Good memories bubbled through Phoebe's mind and popped open with welcoming pieces of happiness as she expertly drove her car along the winding lanes, towards Sennen. She allowed them to continue, the darkness of the saddest day seemed to be fast asleep in her memories. She would tiptoe around it, leaving it undisturbed.

Phoebe thought back to the days when Chesten would go down to the harbour at Sennen, to watch the catch being unloaded. Being the practical girl she was, Tom had taught her many of the skills needed to skipper a boat, she was particularly adept at helping to hoist the containers onto the harbour side and prepare the vessel for the next outing. She was a fast learner, and although a mere slip of a girl she had developed a wiry strength. Whenever her homework was completed, and Sam didn't need her help with the cows, Chesten would ask her mother if she could visit grandad. Phoebe knew that Tom had been the favourite grandparent, but she didn't object. The pair had been a good match, having so much in common with each other. It was a short drive to Sennen and either Phoebe or Tom had willingly picked her up whenever they received the phone call.

Both granddaughters shared the same bedroom at Tumble Down Cottage and were always made welcome when they visited. It was their mother's old room. Tiny in size but with a big heart, the room held a fascination for the girls, especially Chesten. The bedroom window faced the small harbour, which was always a hive of activity, with the local fishermen buzzing around, chatting, sharing biscuits and coffees and sometimes working. From here her granddaughters could see the winch dragging the boats along the beach towards the slipway and beyond that the lifeboat station. The local volunteers would often come down to clean the lifeboat and make sure it was well maintained. You never know when it will be needed, their grandad had told them. The whole harbour was a friendly, busy, tightly knit community. Phoebe knew it was a place Chesten loved to be a part of.

Often pleading with her grandad to take her out on *Pheebz*, Tom had rarely refused. Chesten had been good company for Tom and became animated whenever she was aboard the boat. Spending many hours together, sailing the North Cornwall coast, they had laid the foundations for a strong relationship with each other and the sea. Of course, Tom had loved Tamara, he couldn't have possibly chosen one over the other. But Tamara often chose to follow her mother into her workshop, preferring the lure of clay and glazes instead of boats and the sea.

Phoebe understood that most of the coastal children developed a love of the sea and sailing, and Tamara was no different, but with Chesten it was a passion. As a child, Edith had never shown much interest in the sea, but she didn't prevent her daughters spending time with their grandad and learning from him. Edith had always been a thoughtful person and reasoned any knowledge or skills acquired would be useful someday. The girls were growing up and their interests and personalities were flowing in different directions, like rip currents in the sea.

Pheebz was Chesten's all-time favourite boat, she loved the old wooden fishing vessel. Possibly because of the familiarity of her. Or perhaps it was because she had procured her grandad's undivided attention when they had been on the boat together. *Maybe a bit of both*, thought Phoebe. Chesten declared she was the best boat in the world. Tom had said that their granddaughter was becoming at home on the sea and had admitted to allowing Chesten to skipper the vessel on a few occasions. He had proudly stated that she was a natural. Phoebe knew that he had been amazed at Chesten's prowess of the sea: she had been the apple of his eye.

As Phoebe drew closer to Sennen she began to feel relaxed and contented, as the happy memories flowed through her, and the menacing clouds stayed hidden.

The Saddest Day

On that fateful day, Tom had needed to pick up supplies for his fishing vessel from the ship maintenance shop in Fowey and had left his two employees to fish alone. They were capable lads and would enjoy the independence of the day without their skipper on board. Normally he would send one of them to Fowey for supplies, but it had been a good day for the boys to gain some experience of working under their own judgement. The weather had been fine and the sea was calm; a slow, lazy, late summer morning. He knew the boys would be safe without him. And he would enjoy the slow drive along the narrow, twisting roads. It would allow him time to think about his life — which was good. Being a grandad suited him, and he loved to spend time with Chesten and Tamara.

As Tom travelled to Fowey the road was quiet and relatively traffic free, which was unusual during the summer months when tourist traffic would wander around aimlessly, searching for elusive beaches and secluded villages. Random thoughts skittered around lazily and one settled like a butterfly on a leaf, he wondered where it had been lured from. He hadn't thought about young Michael in years. It was quite a while ago, every spare minute the young lad had he would come down to the harbour to help the fishermen unload their catch. He never seemed to tire of their stories, antics and humour. He loved the sea, but his father had different ideas and persuaded his son to move away, go to college and get a profession. He didn't want his son to become a slave to the sea. *It was just different perspectives*, thought Tom. He had never felt himself to be a slave, more a companion. The fishermen encouraged the boy to take his father's advice, they weren't there to cause family rifts, and perhaps it was for the best. They didn't see much of him after he left for college, but Tom heard that after graduation Michael had returned to someplace in Cornwall and set up a business, something to do with law. Tom wished him well, the lad had always been a quick learner and would make a success of his new venture.

Swinging the car around a sharp corner he saw two leverets on his side of the lane, play boxing. They were too young to realise the danger of the road. Startled by the truck engine they turned and stood perfectly still, fixing Tom with a hypnotic stare. Instinctively Tom swerved onto the right-hand side of the road in an effort to avoid them, unfortunately, at the same time, a car came around the blind bend heading straight towards him. He could see the young family in the car shriek with horror as his truck hurtled towards them. Yanking the steering wheel further right Tom narrowly avoided the family but crashed into an ancient oak tree. His last thoughts, as his life ended, were of his family; Edith, Chesten and Tamara and the girl he loved...Phoebe.

Frustrating and confusing tourists was a game all piskies loved to play but on that day the game had been taken too far. From early morning the three young piskies had mischievously turned signposts around leading tourist traffic up farm lanes that headed nowhere. The tourists relied heavily on road maps and local signposts, having learnt from experience not to trust sat-nav to find any remote place in Cornwall; it didn't work. On that day vehicles became trapped in rutted roads, punctured tyres prevented families from reaching their dream destinations and angry farmers ordered holiday makers off their land. Causing vehicles to slavishly follow circular routes leading them back to their starting points, the three young, pesky piskies fell to the ground in hysterical laughter as they watched the bewildered tourists finally abandon their day trip. The drivers and families argued amongst themselves, and as tempers frayed, they blamed each other for being lost. It was supposed to be harmless fun, but perhaps it was a little cruel when they witnessed children crying with the boredom of riding around all morning in a car travelling nowhere with their parents yelling at each other, apportioning blame. The piskies were young, barely entering adolescence, and becoming unruly. Some said they needed extra guidance from a pack of elders. Obviously just having one mentor wasn't working. On the saddest day, they had sneaked away from the tribe and were unsupervised. They were taking measures to the extreme, but being juvenile and thoughtless they were goading each other to take even more risks.

Believing the repositioned signpost to be correct the driver had eagerly turned onto the twisting lane, which was well known by the locals as one way. He was weary of the constant dead ends and farm lanes he had mistakenly taken to be the much sought-after route to the beach. The driver tried to add a little cheer into the car by encouraging the children to look out for the sea.

The three young piskies watched captivated as the unsuspecting vehicles headed towards each other. The blind bend in the lane was going to be the point where the motorists first caught sight of each other. It would be fun to see the panic on their faces as the vehicles swerved frantically to avoid each other. Hardly able to conceal their mirth, they crouched down in the undergrowth to watch the play unfold. Recklessly, the leader of the threesome came up with a brilliant idea and set a pair of leverets in the bend of the road to practise play boxing. Tempting them with the promise of where to find the most luscious grass in North Cornwall, if they put on a good show, the young hares took up the challenge. The leverets would cause one more problem for the vehicles, this was going to be an interesting scene to watch.

Car tyres screeched, the leverets froze in panic, and the truck swerved out of control. The high pranks of the morning took on a new dimension; they didn't intend this to happen. The leverets pelted away through the thick hedgerow and across the open field. At an impressive speed they flew past a piskie elder, who had been snoozing in the shade of an old elm tree warmed by the summer sun. They carried on running even when he called for them to stop, fearing they might become associated with any of the morning's happenings. The screeching of tyres and the sickening crash which followed, plus the groaning and crying of the ancient oak tree had rudely awakened him.

Patting the old elm and thanking him for his hospitality, he marched off across the field to investigate what had happened. He had a sickening feeling that the troublesome threesome, as the tribe had named them, would have something to do with it. Being responsible for their apprenticeship was a chore, they were getting to be too much of a handful; he would hand their training over to some other member of the tribe. He was tired of constantly checking on the level of mischief they were creating and reminding them repeatedly of the tribe's ethos; mischief and trickery. It was a fine line which could be easily stepped over, then you were left with chaos and calamity. When he saw the devastation, he scolded the trio and quickly made sure all was made well. He supervised while the youngsters scrambled around correcting the signposts, then banished them back into the woodlands and undergrowth. He hastily checked on Tom, maybe there was something he could do. The piskies weren't there to cause death and destruction.

Sadly, he saw Tom was dying; there was nothing he could do as the process had become irreversible. He saw the life force gushing out of him, too fast and furious to stem. Kneeling next to him he held Tom's hand, to comfort him, as the last vestiges of his life blended with the summer air and the essence of him was freed from its bodily constraints.

Sirens screeched in the still air as a police car came speeding to the accident. The piskie elder deemed it time to leave the place and slipped away into the undergrowth. He heard the distraught driver from the family telling the police the one-way sign had definitely not been there, being a very careful motorist, he would have seen the sign. Sighing, and dismally shaking his head, he witnessed an ambulance arriving. *It was too late for that*, he thought.

The elder had recognised Tom, he had played quite a few tricks on him in his time. Tom had always taken the pranks in the manner they were delivered, knowing the piskies meant no harm; they were just fooling around with him. Hiding car keys, stalling the engine of his fishing vessel, cutting his fishing nets, scribing the name on his first boat. Sometimes, Tom had grown angry and shouted abuse at the piskies, but eventually he had quietened down and accepted the joke, often joining in their laughter and appreciating their humour. It was part of being Cornish. No doubt about it, Tom had been a good man and would be missed: devastation had been caused here today. Deep in contemplation as he walked into the woods, he wondered what Tom had meant as the life drained from him. Why did he whisper on his dying breath — *Pheebz,* we have a job to do?

As Phoebe swung her car into the driveway of her cottage, she wiped her eyes. The happy reflections had been wiped away by sad, sad memories that had been disturbed and began to rage through her mind. Wave after wave of sorrow drenched her cherished recollections, and they drowned in a pool of despair. Her recall of the saddest day was still filled with questions: it would never make any sense to her. It was pointless replaying the police report and the driver's account over and over again, but it was the only scant information available. She knew parts of this story were missing, as she tried unsuccessfully to piece together her husband's last moments. Her background in journalism persisted in tormenting her, niggling her with unanswered questions, urging her to delve deeper, but what was the point? She had still lost Tom.

As she opened the wooden door leading into Tumbledown Cottage, its warm comforting arms embraced her. Phoebe felt the affectionate welcome of her home and sighed; she was relieved to be there. It was here where she could finally find peace and relax as the happy memories seeped out of the walls, saturating her thoughts and gaining dominance over her sorrow. The assembly, and the recollections of the saddest day had exhausted her. It was time to rest; let the younger generation deal with life's problems. She could only offer advice now, if anyone would listen.

She smiled as she quietly said hello to Tom. As if in

answer, she was sure that she sensed the warmth of the sunshine and the smell of the sea that always followed him around.

As Busy As A Bee

Rupert was renowned for his prompt and efficient handling of projects he was in charge of. Within twenty-four hours he had organised a plan of action for entry into the sealed off undersea tin mine. His plan consisted of: official and local colleagues who were able to discuss strategies and take action, his select unit and a team of local volunteers whom he considered adept to enter the mine, protective equipment for the team, communication devices, lighting to illuminate the mine and specialised equipment to force entry into the sealed area. As Rupert mentally ticked off the list in his head, he saw Bridget and Phil arrive, they acknowledged Rupert with a wave and headed straight towards the marquee, his temporary headquarters. He breathed a sigh of relief, knowing his capable friends would lighten the burden for him.

In order to gain a balanced view of the project, Rupert had recruited a couple of MoD officials, who were also his close friends, Bridget and Phil. They would run the operation from the headland while the team entered the mine, acting as advisors. Rupert knew they were well suited to this role being good listeners and creative thinkers. He glanced over to the marquee, which was being set up on the headland: this would be the hub of the operation and would house all the communication equipment. Bridget was already supervising the installation of a telephone line, the mobile signal on the headland was notoriously unreliable. Phil was making himself busy checking over the walkie talkies, which would be needed when they entered the mine. Rupert was pleased to see his good friends taking control of the situation. He had chosen well.

Rupert had actively encouraged local people to come forward and offer valuable insight into the workings and configuration of the mine. He realised the information they had, concerning the mine and the storage of the tanks, was essential to the successful outcome of the project. Without local help it would be like working blindfolded. From his own experiences, and counsel passed down to him, he knew the value of their input and the catastrophic effect of ignoring it.

Major Angove needed to verify if there was a fracture in the wall of the mine. Quite possibly, as boys, they had panicked and embellished what they had seen. While he was there, he would also monitor the general structure and safety of the mine. If all was well his team would try to locate the tanks and the specialist unit would check they were still fit for purpose; scrutinise them for damage and leakage.

Looking at his grandfather George's map of the mine, he could envisage where the tanks were stored. If they continued along the main tunnel, he wasn't exactly sure how far, he felt confident they would be found there. The site was pinpointed on the map with skull and crossbones and had been sealed off from the rest of the mine. Hand drawn by his grandfather, the map was detailed and fascinating. Rupert had often sat down at night after supper and, armed with the old map, had perused the tunnels that wormed their way under the Cornish seabed. Rupert had taken it upon himself to memorise every twist, turn and dead end in the tunnel. He knew that one day he would be entering the mine again, and this time he would make sure he was able to walk out… even in the dark.

As Sam and Jasper arrived, they found Rupert on Botack Headland together with all the entourage involved with operation Tidy Up, as Jasper had named it. Major Angove was instructing his unit on the course of action they were about to undertake, and the importance of the team of the four local men and women who would accompany them. He had chosen his unit for their bravery, intelligence and ability to listen and form opinions from the information presented to them, from whatever source. He knew the value of listeners over talkers, one was only able to learn if one was willing to listen. They all had a good track record — successfully working together on numerous varied and dangerous assignments and performing excellently on many occasions that Rupert had headed. All of the members of the unit had one thing in common, something Rupert believed to be of great importance in this assignment: they all originated from towns and villages on the coast. In his experience coastal dwellers viewed life differently from inland people. They were more attuned to nature and her quick, uncontrollable transitions. Realising some things were out of their control, they quickly accepted the fact and worked alongside the chaos to try to turn it to their advantage. Inland people tended to be under the misconception that control could be achieved in any situation: it was an illusion.

Sam was watching all the busy activity around the entrance; he was eager to enter the mine. He needed to put an end to the chaos that was seeping into their lives. Unfortunately, this morning, another one of his calves had become lame. Time was running out, they needed to take immediate action. He had been chosen to be part of the team as Rupert knew him to be a self-disciplined, proactive person who would take charge if need be.

Jasper would also form part of this group. He was no longer the scared little boy who had entered the mine thirty years ago, but a strong determined man who had an uncanny relationship with nature and wildlife. Rupert knew Jasper's presence was vital to the success of the operation, if there was any truth in the Dragon's existence Jasper would be needed to summon her help… or for protection against her. He wouldn't allow himself to take his team into the undersea tin mine with the possibility of an unpredictable Dragon only metres away — without Jasper there to appease her.

Eleanor and her sister Anna had also arrived at the scene. With trepidation, Eleanor had conceded to be part of the operation. Rupert felt that she would be a valuable member of the team with her strange ability to see occurrences that were obscured from others. Anna, with her down to earth reasoning and soothing manner would be there to pacify her sister, if the stress became too great for her.

Within an hour of arriving at the mine, Major Angove was informed by his technicians that the entrance was open; they had broken the lock. The tin mine was ready to be entered. He wondered who had repaired it after Jasper had broken it thirty years ago? No one had informed him of any report, official or unofficial, about the lock being broken… or repaired. It didn't make any sense. He pushed the thoughts away and concentrated on the present. He could ponder about the past when the operation was completed.

Rupert and the MoD officials made a final check, making sure everyone was wearing protective clothing and breathing apparatus was at hand. As they entered the mine the technicians fixed lighting along the damp concrete walls. Rupert didn't savour the prospect of being plunged into total darkness again. In the stark, bright light the tin mine took on a less threatening appearance, which visibly relaxed the team. As they proceeded, and Eleanor began talking to a young female officer, Kate, the atmosphere began to warm. Both army personnel and locals were bonding to form one team.

The Other Sister

Anna took advantage of the conversation between Eleanor and Kate to find time to mull over her own thoughts. Eleanor could be draining at times with her intensity, nevertheless Anna always managed to find some inner strength to deal with her. The blazing electric lights provided adequate illumination for the old mine, but Anna could still see intimidating corners filling up with menacing shadows. The light was unable to penetrate everywhere. What lurked in their blackness, she wondered? At times she saw, or perhaps imagined, a movement, but she wasn't certain. Could it be her mind playing tricks, or was there some kind of animal moving along… slowly… following them? She was unable to grasp hold of a shape or an outline when she looked directly at the shadows, it was her peripheral vision that caught the slight movements which suggested a form. No one else seemed to notice, or feel, the animosity that was hiding behind a sugary cloak, not even Eleanor who was still chatting with Kate. She noticed her sister seemed too relaxed, too at ease, not herself; something was wrong. As they reached the steep slope, which descended into the bowels of the mine, it became difficult for her to maintain a balanced gait. A kind young sergeant, Evan, took hold of her arm and held her steady. She thanked him and politely dismissed him when the slope levelled out. Revelling in the freedom of being alone with her thoughts she didn't intend striking up a meaningless conversation with a stranger. An awareness gently rippled over her, infiltrating her body, she was familiar with the feeling. A warning to be alert of anything unusual. It was like the whispering of the sea caressing smooth pebbles, the lull before the storm. The notion made her laugh... everything was unusual in this alien environment! Perhaps she was overreacting.

Realising she was under the sea, when she heard the heavy boulders being dragged along the seabed, was unsettling. *The ocean must be particularly choppy this morning*, she thought. *Or maybe it was like this all the time.* The noise was deafening and constricted her thoughts. Furthermore, the protective clothing was tiring and restricted her movements. Everything seemed to be tightening, compressing and contracting around her. How much further would they be progressing? As if in answer to her question Rupert announced to the group that the junction was a few metres ahead. This was where the boys had first seen the crack in the wall — all those years ago. This was where Jasper had made contact with the Dragon and summoned up the anger and hatred of the piskie. This was where they had been plunged into darkness and struggled to find their way out of the mine. She shook herself in an attempt to dismiss the negative mindset, in the hope of gaining a grip on reality. She was with an expert army unit, headed by Rupert. Technicians were constantly working away assessing the safety of the mine, stringing up lights and checking on the air quality. Her friends and sister were here with her. What could go wrong?

Major Angove was pleased. Everything was going as planned. He hadn't expected things to run quite so smoothly. They were nearing the site where they had seen the fracture in the wall when they were boys. If it was there, they would inspect the damage. If it was safe, they would proceed to locate the tanks and assess their state of repair. Glancing around to check on the progress of the group, Rupert could see Kate was chatting with Eleanor. Kate knew how to make people relax and would be able to gather valuable local information from her. The other sister was standing slightly away from the group. He had seen Evan trying to talk to her earlier, but she didn't reciprocate. After a while Evan had left her alone.

Rupert was positive that Anna must be enjoying the freedom of her own company, however short it might be. She had spent years of her life caring for her sister. He wondered how she managed to live such a selfless, small life. Surely at some point she would break free. He noted she appeared agitated and had the look of a startled roe deer, and she was supposed to be the down to earth one. He would tell young Evan to keep an eye on her. In his experience it was the quiet ones who always caused the most trouble.

Other members of his unit had sought a local to befriend and conversations were flowing. Rupert was satisfied with his unit; he had chosen well. The technicians were working a few metres in front of the main group, quickly and efficiently stringing up lights to illuminate their way: beckoning the group forward. Rupert rationalised that maybe they had overreacted all those years ago when they entered the mine, after all, they had only been young boys.

Jasper broke away from the group and headed towards the crack: it was there and it had widened. He placed his hand on the wall and felt the slight tremble of the concrete as the boulders scraped along the seabed, reminding him that the ocean was close by, eager to storm in, if someone would open the door. Sam and

Rupert also joined Jasper to inspect the fault, they were the only ones who were able to compare the damaged wall with its condition thirty years ago. The only ones who could say whether nor not it had deteriorated. Sea water was seeping into the mine through the fault. The old original wooden wall, hidden behind the concrete, could be seen when a light was shone into the crack. *Porous rocks must be present at this site, probably granite*, Jasper thought. Over a long period of time the rocks would allow a steady trickle of water to enter the mine. He imagined the sea water snaking its way through the rocks, crevices and old wood, enabling it to wear down the reinforced concrete. Hardly surprising after all this time. The mine hadn't been serviced or repaired in over a hundred years, not since it had been locked down. Everything disintegrates with age, and it was time to sort out those tanks. *If the walls could start to crumble here, then why not where the gas was stored?* They needed to press on.

Rupert was eager to make more progress and when the wall passed the safety check, as he was sure it would, they would continue along the passage and locate the tanks. When they reached the sealed off area and gained entry, his unit would examine the tanks: check for leakage and security, and if they were still fit for purpose. It would be a good day's work achieved, and decisions would be made on their next course of action.

Sam thought that maybe as young boys they had panicked at the sight of the leakage when they had imagined that the sea was going to rush in and claim them. The idea had been intensified by the piskie, who had fed fear and anxiety into their receptive minds. That wouldn't happen today; they knew exactly what they were doing.

When Rupert and his technicians had completed their inspection, Anna walked up to the fault and placed her palm on the wall. No one noticed her, she had that way — a cloak of invisibility thrown over her by her sister's needs. With the tips of her fingers, she traced its outline, cutting her index finger on the crumbling concrete. A few drops of blood dripped into the fault and mixed with the salty sea water causing it to change from bright sticky red to inconspicuous sickly pink. *Just like herself,* she thought bitterly. She sucked her finger to stem the flow of blood and the sharp metallic taste felt good. It proved she was living. Sometimes, she wasn't sure: her life had become so insignificant. She could sense a presence on the other side of the wall, a ghost of a presence. Whatever had been there had recently withdrawn, leaving behind a memory of faltering movements and failing strength. It was a sea creature and Anna felt an affinity towards it. Her blood quickened; she was beginning to feel alive.

Into Madness

As mad as a hatter. As sour as vinegar. He peevishly hid in the dark, familiar, secret places that comprised the undersea tin mine. By skulking along the walls, he was able to hide his presence and observe the intruders. Twisting and turning his grotesque filthy body, to conceal it from the torturous blazing lights, he trailed the team deep into the mine. What were they up to? He recognised the three intruders from thirty years ago: men now, not boys. Human life was so short, a mere blink of the eye. Yet the time he had spent here, captive, isolated and going mad… it seemed as if he had been banished forever, but it was merely a hundred years. It might be forever, if he was unable to change. *Maybe I could have a little fun here, relieve the boredom,* thought the piskie.

As the years in isolation and incarceration progressed, he found it more and more difficult to alter his mindset: he was unable to make the changes necessary for him to re-join the tribe. Although piskies were allowed to perform mischief and trickery all day long, in fact they were positively encouraged to do so, there were certain rules they had to adhere to. Being unable to follow those fundamental rules, of secrecy and invisibility, had led the errant piskie to reveal the siting of their camp which enraged the elders. They said he had put the whole tribe in danger. He argued that he had inadvertently disclosed its location when he had been chatting with the hares, and who were they going to tell? Nobody! As far as he was concerned, he hadn't put the tribe at any risk. The elders had sighed with frustration, realising they were unable to persuade him to conform to their ideas. He thought that the elders enforced ridiculous rules at times, they were stuck in their ways. The errant piskie was vocal in his opinions, stating that it was time for new blood to enter the leadership as it may offer some joie de vivre to their lives. But the elders were adamant in their thinking saying the tribe remained safe only as long as their presence was shrouded in mystery and superstition and the location of their camp remained a secret. If their existence became common knowledge, they could look forward to becoming a Victorian freak show.

Hastily the tribe had been uprooted and moved to a new location. *Rather an over-the-top reaction*, he thought. Many of the tribe members were reluctant to move and needed some persuading, but they eventually accepted the elders' decision. The tribe had lived in the old place for a long time and considered it to be their home, moving meant change, and the piskies found change unsettling. Resentment grew throughout the tribe as they begrudgingly packed up their belongings and began the exodus. Most of the tribe concluded that the errant piskie was a liability and chose to ignore him. In his opinion the new site was in a much better location so they should be thanking him!

Then a complaint was made against him, from an anonymous source, but he had a good idea who it was, about the death and destruction of a small flock of sheep and a few cattle. He had been seen sprinkling their water troughs with some of the poisonous gas he had acquired before it was sealed in the tin mine. There had only been the old, nosy piskie around that day who could have witnessed his actions — if he ever got out of here, he would deal with him. In his opinion, the animals had taken up far too much space and needed thinning out. Their constant bleating and lowing had caused sleepless nights for some of the piskies, and he knew quite a few of his companions had been pleased when he had put an end to the noise pollution.

Finally, the straw to break the camel's back came when he was accused of pursuing his own idea of fun and games with a total disregard of the tribe's fundamental rules. They said he had potentially exposed the existence of the piskies. Potentially! Well, that wasn't definitely… what on earth was all the fuss about? By refusing to alter his ways and trying to lead some of the younger piskies into his wayward actions, the elders considered him a threat to the very existence of the tribe.

This last misdemeanour had been quite bland, as far as he was concerned. It had started with a normal piskie day, breakfasting together on stodgy gruel; cooked by someone who dared to call herself a chef! Everyone telling the elders how wonderful they were, what amazing decisions they were making — all pretty boring stuff. In an aim to inject some fun into his life he had decided to lead a team of impressionable youngsters into the town centre to cause mischief and trickery, nothing else.

It was the first May Day celebrations after the Great War had ended, and the town would be buzzing with people — the piskie loved a good party. He had been eager to get there. The town was strictly forbidden, out of bounds. The elders reasoned there would be too many people around who might catch sight of them, particularly the younger less experienced piskies who sometimes had trouble with the smoke and mirrors effect.

Blah, blah, blah. He knew all of this, but the town was so enticing, rather like the forbidden fruit in the garden of Eden. It had been a great adventure… and they hadn't been seen. People were far too engrossed in their own mundane lives to notice something that they considered shouldn't be there.

At least he had been able to generate a little spark in his life, unlike the stuffy elders. The youngsters had told him they had enjoyed the adventure and were looking forward to the next one. He loved living life on the edge. Everything had been cleared up, the broken window was put down to a fault in the glass. A young girl had been blamed for the dog being released from his lead, she had cried for hours over that one. The missing wallet from the famer's coat pocket was considered stolen by a pickpocket, it was hilarious. His face had turned purple when he realised his money was missing. No one could point the finger of blame at the piskies, so what was the problem? The elders sighed when they listened to the reasons for his actions, they realised he lived in the moment, didn't consider the outcome of his actions. If they didn't remove him from the tribe there was a danger that he might entice more youngsters to follow his lead, and that could be catastrophic for all of them. The elders believed that the solitude in the undersea tin mine would bring him to his senses, by allowing him time to address his past misdeeds and ask for vindication. They hadn't reckoned on the extent of the errant piskie's dark soul.

The selected pack of elders visited him every decade to question him about his thoughts and ideas, in the hope they would be able to reintegrate him back into the tribe. Sensing a way out of his captivity, he decided to try and trick them into believing he was contrite, willing to change his ways. At first, he had tried to put forward a false persona, sorrowfully brimming with regret at his dark and wicked actions in an effort to regain freedom, but the elders were too smart and could see through his little game. And so, time went on and on and he grew madder and madder; the captivity and isolation weren't working.

A maniacal idea tugged away at him, he had to stifle a hysterical laugh, he didn't want the team to know he was there… not yet. The thought took form. Would it be more fun to cause death and destruction to the men now, at their age, with families that relied on them and old friends who would miss them? They were so easy to fool. Wrapped up in their own small worlds, busy trying to maintain some kind of control and order. He had been using piskie trickery to project a feeling of wellbeing throughout the team. It was easier to scrutinise people when they were relaxed. He noted that everyone here imagined that they were important and indispensable: they were wrong.

At first no one had noticed his presence, but one of them was becoming aware of him, one of them was different. She had spent a lifetime thinking and caring about someone else, so had been granted little time to become preoccupied with herself. She had never been allowed to consider herself; it was always about the other one. He sensed there was some resentment lurking there. There was something familiar in her psyche, she was interesting. Something dark and sinister coated with sugar. He knew she had been watching him but not once did she alert anyone. He took his time to study her movements, her body language and her interactions with the team members. Understanding she was there for one reason, to stabilise her sister if it was necessary, he knew it made her feel worthless. He could feel her questioning herself about her usefulness in life. He could taste her displeasure; it was bitter on his tongue. He knew that at one time she had been loved and valued… many years ago.

Abandoned Love

For Anna it had been a summer of love. A time during the mid-sixties when she had been young and full of dreams, an adolescent girl bordering on womanhood. The days had been hot, thrilling and unforgettably enjoyable. The Cornish sunshine bathed the sea and beaches in glorious warmth from sunrise to sunset. Days were easy, uncomplicated and seemingly never ending, as only the young appreciate. She had never been a beauty. However, with her delicate features and pale skin she was considered pretty by some, but to one she was his Helen of Troy: the most beautiful woman to walk the earth.

The musician had courted her all the long, hot summer days… and nights. He tried to persuade her to travel with him, saying they were going to be famous one day, and she was his muse. Anna was captivated. Never-ending days on the beach, revelling in the joy of being young and favoured, she listened to her musician playing his guitar and singing for their friends and tourists. She became the central theme for his songs, life couldn't get any better than this. As word of his talent grew, crowds of people gathered to appreciate his love songs about the pale, fine featured beauty who had stolen his heart. Anna was thrilled with all the attention and grew in confidence and beauty daily. Her hair shone, her eyes gleamed, and her sun-kissed skin glowed as she felt the acuity of first love.

When he tired of entertaining others, they would swim

in the ocean. At first, Anna had been afraid of the sea, it was too wide, too deep: it would swallow her whole, she confided. As her familiarity of the watery playground grew, with each passing day, he swept away all of her fears and led her deeper and deeper into the undisclosed. She bounded through the waves and tumbled in the surf; she was at home. He laughed at her new-found self and likened her to a mermaid, saying if ever she sang to him, he would become enchanted.

Never having experienced undivided attention in all her life, she had always played second fiddle to her sister's needs, Anna drank greedily from the pool of love and affection presented to her. He promised never to let her go and vowed to love her for all eternity. They lazily made sketchy plans to travel abroad and follow the sun, after the Cornish summer ended. A golden era was opening up for Anna where foreign, exotic places offered a chance for them to live together and be happy, all that was required of her was to say yes. Anna was sold on the idea; she was overwhelmed with his romantic language. At nights, her dreams were full of adventure, freedom and discovery. All too soon the summer ended, and it was time to go.

Her sister, who had relentlessly relied upon her, was distraught — she couldn't live without Anna she declared. Anna tried to reason with her, saying she would return home in a few months, she would always be there for her but needed a little space to venture out on her own… for a short while. Her mother said it was just a summer love affair and wouldn't amount to anything. It would be more sensible to choose a local boy, someone with a reliable job. Her father kept his own counsel; Anna felt that she sensed restlessness and resentment there. Perhaps he had turned his back on a dream and lived to regret his decision.

Summer ended, and the fateful day arrived. Her musician packed his bags and waited hopefully for his pale, delicate love to appear. Time passed, and with a heavy heart he realised that the love of his life had chosen the familiarity of the here and now instead of the promise of an unknown future. Anna was at home sobbing into her pillow trying to console herself. She had made her decision and was staying, with Eleanor: their paths were interwoven and unbreakable. Always being a strange child, her sister weighed Anna down with her dependence upon her. Anna loved Eleanor and had tried to encourage independence in her, but no amount of praise or instruction could release the clam-like clutch she exerted on Anna. It was from that moment the seed of resentment was planted in Anna's brain.

Remembering the day their mother had brought the tiny baby home, a welcome new addition to the family, Anna felt a deep contentment, the baby had been adorable. Eight years her senior, Anna mothered and cared for baby Eleanor when their mother couldn't cope with the constant demands the baby made. It was Anna who would soothe the baby to sleep, tempt her to drink her milk and make new foods for her to try. Over time, the distance between mother and baby drifted further and further apart but between the sisters it grew closer and closer. Anna had never felt such love in her life, and their relationship began to blossom and grow through mutual love and affection. Whenever people passed comments on Eleanor's behaviour not being quite right, being strange or not normal, Anna would jump to her defence stating everyone was different, her sister was fine.

Anna never swam in the ocean again. At night, alone in her bedroom, she would sing quietly to her lost love hoping the enchantment would lure him back to her…

one day. She painfully remembered that her musician did become famous, and many of his songs were about a long-lost love who lived by the sea. As good as they were they didn't bring her any joy or comfort, only a deepening sense of resentment…

Jasper had been unable to find any physical presence of the Dragon, even though he had cleared his mind and sought her movements through the concrete wall. However, he did perceive her recent departure. Before he entered the mine, he had been certain he would connect with her again; it was the reason he had agreed to accompany the unit. He pictured her making her way to the Mermaid Cave as the tide was on the turn. Sam had told him that was her usual routine. Instinctively he had sensed something was wrong with her mobility; the ghost of her departure was jolting instead of being the smooth transition he remembered… it wasn't right. Turning to Sam to voice his concerns he was met with Rupert's confirmation that the fault in the wall was secure, they would be proceeding. Jasper decided to keep his worries to himself, and together with Sam and Rupert they led the team along the passageway heading for the storage area. Like adventurers of long ago they fell into step with each other. According to Rupert's map, he estimated they should only be a few hundred metres from the sealed area of the mine where the tanks were held. This part of the journey was uncharted territory: no one had walked this path in the past hundred years.

The piskie, sensing some loss of control over Anna, quickly diverted his attention back to her, swamping her with negative thoughts. Anna followed the team further and further into the mine. She became intrigued with the prospect of the unknown. She was delving into darkness.

Pheebz

As sharp as a knife, she cut through the calm slack tide of the Atlantic Ocean. Powerful and determined she defied her age, carrying her priceless shipment of Chesten, Tamara and Jack towards their destination — Mermaid Cave. They had decided upon their course of action the day after the assembly at Cove Cottage: Chesten had finally convinced them that the Dragon needed their help. They were animated with the taste of adventure tinged with danger. If nan and grandad could enter Mermaid Cave and save the Dragon, surely the three of them could do the same. Chesten conveniently didn't mention the part that grandad had played in the scenario — that of expert sailor.

Chesten had suggested they take the old boat while Sam and Jasper were preoccupied with re-entering the undersea tin mine; they would be too engrossed in their task to pay much heed of their children's actions. Reluctantly Tamara and Jack agreed it was a good strategy, no one would be around to question what they were doing. *Pheebz* was secured at the harbour and was eager for an outing on the sea, and Chesten was passionate at the prospect of taking her out. Edith would be busy in her workshop and Molly would be tending the sheep. They would have a few hours before anyone noticed their disappearance, by then they would be well on their way to save the Dragon.

Jack felt uncomfortable with the speed of the plan's formation, he wasn't sure they had covered every aspect. Furthermore, he wasn't convinced the Dragon needed rescuing. When she had entered the strait, she looked fit and agile, but the discarded scale did suggest that maybe she was experiencing some lack of condition. Also, the weird happenings around the cove, a possible unbalance of nature… something was amiss there. Admittedly it did point to the Dragon's inability to cope, but surely it would have made more sense to wait a few days to see if the Dragon could manage without their help. When problems arose with the sheep's health or well-being his dad's approach was to give nature a chance to perform her healing powers. Of course, if that didn't work then he would intervene. Chesten wouldn't listen to his logic, she was adamant the Dragon needed her support. He accepted the fact that the quest was going to happen. Sometimes, he reasoned, you had to take risks in life and if the outcome was the Dragon could be helped, if she needed helping, then he was willing to take the risk. Dark thoughts chipped away at the flimsy plan, but all his efforts to persuade Chesten to abandon her mission were rejected, and he was unwilling to let the girls go there alone, without him.

They would have left the harbour and be way out to sea before anyone noticed the boat was missing, Chesten reaffirmed. She would leave a note, for her mum, notifying her of their plans. It wouldn't be read until Edith had finished her work in the pottery, later that afternoon. Their mum would take immediate action and inform the lifeguards… as soon as she read the note.

"So, we manage to navigate into Mermaid Cave, into the Dragon's lair, and the Dragon appears. You're nuts Chesten! What do you think would happen next?" demanded Tamara. "She could tear us to pieces, and we wouldn't be able to do anything about it, we would be trapped there; unable to escape."

"That won't happen," Chesten replied knowingly. "She will remember us, from when nan was there. We have the same bloodline. She won't harm us."

"Oh, so we will be OK, but what about Jack?" Tamara was unwilling to let this line of argument be dismissed.

"I'm sure he will be fine; he will be with us so the Dragon will trust him."

"Bit of a gamble, don't you think?" Tamara persisted. "An animal in pain often acts out of character. The alternative is she may be fine, resent our invasion of her habitat and we're stuck in the cave, with an angry Dragon! Doesn't bear thinking about."

"Jack can make his own mind up," Chesten replied defiantly, "so can you, but I will be going."

Jack was relieved to hear Tamara voicing her doubts, he hoped she would be able to persuade her sister to abandon the crazy plan. Or maybe Tamara would decide not to join them. It would be one less person to worry about. However, he didn't appreciate how close the girls were. Tamara wouldn't allow Chesten to make the journey without her.

On an occasion when Tamara had joined Chesten to visit their grandad, she witnessed her handling *Pheebz* on the open sea. Quite unconcernedly, grandad had handed over the controls to Chesten who had manoeuvred the boat expertly through the open sea. It was a moment that was ingrained in her memory: she was proud of her sister. Later that evening, Chesten had confided in Tamara that their grandad had been teaching her to skipper *Pheebz*. *The three of them worked well together*, thought Tamara.

"I'm coming with you," announced Tamara, as Jack and her sister were loading up the boat. Although she knew the journey would be treacherous, she had every faith in Chesten's seamanship and wasn't going to miss out on the adventure… it was the Dragon part that worried her.

"We should make it to the cave in about fifteen minutes," Chesten shouted above the engine noise.

The old boat sailed proudly through the sea, responding positively to Chesten's touch and instructions. Jack was impressed with her capabilities; the girl never failed to amaze him. Tamara stood beside her sister, in awe of her navigation skills. Their grandad had taught her well.

"Don't look so amazed, Tammy," Chesten said. "The sea is calm, the tide is about to turn, it's the perfect time to enter the cave."

"I'm not," Tamara replied flippantly. "I know you can do it."

Jack checked over the provisions, they had brought ointment from Sam's medication box that was for his herd. Chesten had chosen this one because she had seen it in action. Any skin disorder suffered by the cows; ringworm, parapox, insect bites, was quickly remedied when it was used. It was a leap of faith, but they had to try something. Food — snacks and water to see them over the hours they would be spending in the cave. Blankets and warm clothes — these would be needed to keep the sneaky, chilly breeze at bay which always took people by surprise at Easter time.

Pheebz sped towards Porthenby Island, which grew in size as the young adventurers drew closer: overshadowing them. It took on a new dimension approaching it from the sea; like the unsymmetrical sides of someone's face or the conflicting traits of their personality. An air of menace was presented from this sea facing side, it seemed to issue a warning. A cold shiver ran through Jack as he realised they were approaching the point of no return, but the sisters looked positively animated. He tried his hardest to shrug off the negative thoughts. The morning sun caught the gold outlining the name *Pheebz* and bounced back into the air and sea, the old boat was enjoying her outing. The trio smiled at each other and laughed out loud at the exhilaration of their escapade. They were young, adventurous and carefree… and they were going to save the Dragon. They could save the world if they put their minds to it.

Nearing the maw of the beast, the boat's engine stuttered and cut out, reluctant to take her precious cargo into the body of the cave. Chesten tried to restart the engine, but the old boat refused to comply; she could be stubborn at times. Chesten determinedly fixed the oars into the oarlocks. Jack hastily sat down next to her and grabbed hold of one of the oars.

"It'll be more difficult if both of us row, we've never practised together," Chesten reasoned. "Leave it to me."

"Move over Jack," Tamara interrupted. "I've had plenty of practise."

Jack reluctantly passed the oar to Tamara, and the two girls slowly rowed the boat through the entrance, into the cave. Tamara concentrated hard, listening to and following her sister's instructions. Jack remained silent, allowing them to focus on synchronising their rowing action: they were perfect. They carefully picked up on the incoming tide which guided them into Mermaid Cave and rowed the boat gently to a small ledge of rocks at the back of the cave. The sisters smiled at each other; they could do this… together. Leaping off the boat, Chesten held her hand out to help Tamara and Jack disembark.

Looking around the cave and taking in their bearings

they were overwhelmed with the beauty that surrounded them. The high domed roof was alive with busy seabirds that had made their nests high and safe from the sea. Their constant toing and froing, in order to find food for their nestlings, was hypnotic to watch. By now the flood tide was beginning to pour into the cave, showering the walls with its foamy white sea spray, creating an illusion of soft billowy clouds. The spring sunshine skipped across the shifting sea that swirled around in the cave, drawing attention to the many ledges and natural steps which would enable the threesome to climb higher to avoid the flood tide. Energy and life were abundant in this abode.

"I need to sketch this," Tamara broke the spell which had enveloped them all. Chesten and Jack laughed at her declaration.

"You will," Chesten said. "As soon as we return home."

After making sure the boat was secure, Jack took the lead and started to climb up to the high ledge that Phoebe had told the girls about. Chesten had said they would be safe there as the flood tide wouldn't reach that far.

Understanding the dangers they faced if they attempted to navigate out of the cave, the decision had been made to stay put, the lifeguards would rescue them. The consequence of their action was something they would have to face. Quite a few of the local teenagers had been caught out by the changeable North Cornwall tides; they wouldn't be the first who needed help. Chesten's grandad had taught her, from an early age, how to read the tide times and also to know the rip currents that wove their way throughout the sea. Always check on the weather, he had stated when she had pleaded for a day on the sea with *Pheebz*. It might look fine but you don't know what's over the horizon; the weather forecast is your best friend. Chesten had completed all those checks, she wasn't going to take Tamara and Jack out onto the open sea if she thought it would endanger their lives. Undeniably, exiting Mermaid's Cave was a different matter, she knew they would need help. Being rescued was a small but embarrassing price to pay if they managed to save the Dragon.

Darkness Prevails

Upon reaching the closed doors, Rupert instructed his technicians to break the seal. He was certain this was where the tanks would be stored. He would enter the area, with his unit, check to make sure they were undamaged and not leaking. For safety reasons, only his specialist unit was allowed past this point; they were stepping into the unknown. Who knew what dangers lurked there? Rupert realised the irony of his decision; the whole mine was unsafe. He had to acknowledge that but still… in his mind the sealed off area posed more of a threat. He had wondered about this area for a long time and now he was going to face his demons…whatever they were.

Instructing his unit to put on their breathing equipment, he prepared to enter the area. The technicians had difficulty opening the door, which creaked and groaned with lifetimes of neglect. Rust, dust and years of accumulated concrete powder fell to the floor as it swung open in a large arc, allowing the unit to enter quickly. The door was closed behind them, with a sickening thud which reverberated throughout the mine but not before the piskie had slipped in.

It was as quiet as a crypt inside the area; no one had placed a foot inside the place for over a hundred years. What would they find? Rupert looked around and with swift efficiency checked on the state of his unit — they were all fine. Armed with ultra-bright powerful LED torches they made their way through the zone, sweeping the torch beams along the walls, roof and floor of the long-abandoned space, checking on the structure, searching for the tanks. Rupert wondered how many metres below the Cornish seabed they were, not many if the deafening sound of the rolling boulders scraping along the seabed was anything to go by. Better not to think about it. This was where the mine ended, a place no one would choose to be. Several torch beams converged on one point, at the far end of the cordoned off area. They had found their prize, six metal tanks, innocent looking containers stacked against the far wall. They looked abandoned. The mistakes, errors and offences of their forefathers needed to be rectified.

Forsaken for over a hundred years, the tanks were saddened at their fragility and inability to remain fit for purpose. They didn't intend to release their deadly contents and haunt this new generation, but nothing remains the same forever. The piskie felt the sadness leaking out of the tanks, feeling justifiably annoyed that the humans had placed such a burden on them. It was an unrealistic task they had been set.

The piskie had always wondered what the sealed off area contained, and now he was face to face with the curiosity. Sliding around the back of the tanks, he examined the seals and joints tutting to himself at the poor state of them. He reasoned that the problem with humans was they lived in the present, they didn't think long-term. He wondered why anyone would produce such a toxic gas, and then try and store it here, under the sea, forever… it was insane. This long-abandoned substance was managing to leak into the sea, it would cause chaos and calamity throughout their region. A far reach from the piskie motto of mischief and trickery. The piskie stopped and checked himself. What was wrong with him?

The strange woman, Anna, they called her. She had altered something deep in him. He was beginning to understand cause and effect, right and wrong, good and bad. It was a strange, unpleasant feeling, a changing process within himself. Piskies found change unsettling.

He didn't like the three boys. They had been too cocksure. They had blundered into his mine and disturbed his mindset with their air of freedom and adventure. He had been certain that he had taught them a short, sharp lesson, all those years ago, but obviously not — they were here again. Unwelcome. No longer fledglings but fully grown. Their grouping posed a new problem, he sensed their power. *The threesome had become a triumvirate: the pragmatist, the storyteller and the animal whisperer*, he thought bitterly. He wouldn't be able to cause much distress to them now; his power was diminished against their joined strength. Strangely, the idea seemed to become less and less of a bother to him. Maybe together, the three men would be able to sort this problem. He hoped so.

It was too immense for the Dragon, that was for sure; she was failing. She had been trying to neutralise the effects of the gas as it leaked into the sea, but the outcome of her actions was destroying her. He understood that now.

He had been trying to find out what she had been up to for months, but she was unwilling to share anything with him; she didn't trust him. He had been disloyal. They had lost their friendship somewhere along the way; he regretted the loss. He considered their disagreement trivial, but the Dragon had been adamant, and he was unwilling to apologise. By sensing her movements in the sea, he had been able to follow her up and down the mine. She had spent an excessive amount of time around the sealed area, and now the mystery was solved. A feeling of sadness trickled into him. If only she could have shared her problem with him. He wouldn't have been able to help clear the mess, but she could have confided in him, which always helps.

Rupert's unit was busy inspecting the tanks; they didn't waste time. Kate and Evan were working together, they had identified a fault in one of the tanks. It was minute but large enough to allow some of the gas to seep through. On close inspection an imperceivable faint green haze could be seen bubbling through one of the joints on the base of a tank. The rest of the tanks appeared to be safely holding their toxic load. Rupert knew they had to be removed, he couldn't risk leaving them here. If one of the tanks was faulty, maybe due to the metal corroding, then the others would probably follow suit. They inspected the floor, walls and roof of the enclosed area searching for faults or cracks which may allow the gas to seep through and potentially make its way into the ocean. Evan spotted two possible regions, which were adjacent to the damaged tank.

"Sir. This could be where the gas leaks into the sea," announced Evan.

Rupert stared at the faults in the wall, imagining the gas winding its way through the narrow region between tunnel wall and open sea. Like a slithering green snake moving towards its prey. The notion made him shudder. If a small amount of gas leakage, such as was present at the moment, could cause the damage they had witnessed in the locality then what would happen if the load increased? It was a shocking image.

"I can confirm that Sir," Kate stated. "It seems likely we have found our weak spot."

There was no time to waste, immediate action needed

to be taken. Rupert thought grimly that it was a Catch-22 situation. If they left the tanks alone, and made safe the area that contained them, over time more tanks may rupture, more cracks could appear in the concrete, and then the poisonous gas would be able to make its way into the sea… again. It was a short-term answer. If they tried to remove the tanks, due to their age and the decomposition of the metal the tanks were constructed from, they could rupture. This would allow the gas to flood throughout the mine and escape along the long tunnel leading outside into the pure Cornish air. He instructed his team that they would secure the door and leave the mine immediately to plot the next course of action. He had already made his decision — the gas would be removed.

As they opened the door and stepped out of the area to re-join the team, Anna noticed the piskie slither out of the chamber and scurry away into his familiar dark places. She was standing alone, lost in her thoughts, staring at a single white feather suspended in the air. She wondered where it had come from and why it remained stationary. When the old vault door had opened and created a sudden rush of fetid air into the mine, it had remained in the same position, still, unmoving. This wasn't right. She reached out to touch it, and as her finger felt its soft edge, she experienced a crashing of the dark and dismal clouds that had fogged her brain. She was returning to her former self, the real Anna. She was in control of herself again. The team responded in various ways with each member shaking off the blanket of illusion that had swaddled them. Their senses and instincts were reinstated, and an awareness of threat and danger presented itself. It circled mischievously around them. The piskie's trick was collapsing, he had managed to maintain it for a surprisingly long time. Smoke and mirrors were being swept away. By creating a false sense of well-being throughout the team he had lured them deep into the tin mine, to the very heart of it, with his intention of preventing them from leaving. As the feather floated to the ground, they heard the maniacal laugh of the piskie, it was spine chilling. At that moment the mine was plunged into darkness so deep and impenetrable it appeared unworldly. The piskie had torn down the lead that fed the lights with power. Starved of their energy source, the lifeless bulbs were unable to illuminate the way home. *Time for the light to sleep and the darkness to prevail*, thought the piskie. He couldn't help himself. It was mischief and trickery — an inherent part of him.

A Sorry Sight

Reaching the high ledge of Mermaid Cave had been relatively easy for the threesome. They were young, fit and agile and charged with adrenalin. Chatting among themselves they were beginning to form a bond; a new grouping was developing. Tamara had to consider that Jack, quite possibly, offered a new dimension to her relationship with Chesten, easing the intensity between the two sisters.

For as long as Tamara could remember, it had always been the two of them... Chesten and Tamara. She liked this team. Of course, there were times when she chose to be with her own friends, to hang out with them, be part of the gang. Other times she would choose to be with her mother, following Edith's every move as she transformed the clay into various art forms on her potter's wheel. How could she not watch as the performer completed such amazing tasks? With her mother's encouragement Tamara was motivated to build her own creations, Edith even allowed her daughter to use the wheel which was out of bounds to anyone else. Her love of art was nourished by Edith's support, and from a young age Tamara would examine, touch, and experience all the wonderful materials and tools that lived in the workshop. Her mother said she was a natural artist, far more talented than she could ever be. Tamara revelled in the compliments and strived to improve her work which, as she grew into adolescence, led her along a different path and away from Chesten.

It was a gradual growth that both sisters accepted. Maybe the times they spent apart served to deepen their sibling bond. Tamara knew one thing for certain, it was much more enjoyable than joining Chesten on her visits to their grandad. Not that she didn't love grandad, but she knew they were just messing around with boats, and she had outgrown that interest. At times she would accompany her sister, feeling the need to see their grandad, nan and Tumbledown Cottage, although her preference was her mother's workshop — it was an Aladdin's Cave.

The silences in the newly formed group became comfortable, their interactions more familiar, less forced. Tamara poured everyone a cup of coffee to pass the time as they waited for the Dragon to appear, or maybe not. By now the flood tide was rushing in through the entrance, bouncing off the steep walls, creating swirls of tumultuous water which caused *Pheebz* to knock against the cave's walls. Chesten looked worried when she saw the tiny boat take hit after hit on the hard granite rock. She was like a thing possessed. *It was a good job she had tied the boat securely,* Chesten thought, *otherwise she would have been smashed to pieces.*

"Look!" yelled Jack, drawing Chesten and Tamara's attention to the mouth of the cave.

And there she was. Riding in on the flood tide. The reality of seeing the sea monster heading towards them caused the three teenagers to group together for support. Although they knew the Dragon from stories, this was a completely different experience and fear warned them of their precarious situation. Gradually, as the Dragon neared the back of the cave it became clearer to them: she was a creature in need of help. She appeared tired, old and worn out, a sorry sight. They stood helpless as the poor beast dragged herself onto a lower ledge, utterly depleted and gasping for breath. She lifted her once majestic head and saw the trio above her. Chesten was sure she saw a hint of recognition in those dull, ancient eyes. Slowly the Dragon made her way up to the high ledge, stumbling over loose rocks and slippery ledges, it was juxtaposed with the ascent the threesome had made.

"Come on girl. You can do it," Jack urged soothingly, realising the Dragon meant them no harm.

Finally, the Dragon reached the high ledge and with one last, great effort she heaved herself up and slumped down on the rock: her lair. Chesten and Jack moved slowly and gently to her side, all fear of the Dragon had dissipated and was carried away in the sea mist. They were practised at moving around sick animals and knew how to calm her. Tamara, gaining confidence from her sister's demeanour, opened the jar and passed the ointment to her. Peering into the open jar Chesten was despondent, realising her gesture would be insufficient. How could such a small token save this huge animal? Scrutinising the Dragon's vast body Chesten and Jack worked together, as a team. They worked quietly and efficiently, relentlessly searching for positive signs that meant the Dragon would recover; that she would live. They were engrossed in their work and time slipped by as Tamara watched, and the cave filled with the sea.

"We'll try the ointment," Chesten said dismally.

"It will work. I'm sure," Tamara said, trying to lift her sister's spirit.

Jack watched hopefully while Chesten massaged the ointment into the torn, ragged, worn-out scales.

The Dragon sighed with relief as the ointment was soaked up by her body, she appeared to be gaining some ease from her condition. When the task was completed Chesten gently placed her head against the Dragon's, with the hope of strengthening their connection and allowing the Dragon's spirit to enter her body as she left her earthly constraints. The Dragon's eyes were dimmed and tired, she needed to rest, for a long time. Although it was plain to see she was dying, Chesten was adamant the decision to save her had been the right one — she was able to offer comfort as the Dragon's life slipped away. Jack sat next to Chesten and gently stroked the top of the Dragon's head. Both of them had the knowledge and experience of animals being in pain and dying, they would maintain their vigil for however long it lasted. Working with cows and sheep since a very young age they knew this part of life was unavoidable; the ending. The Dragon had worked ceaselessly to protect the flora and fauna around Porthenby, it was the least they could do.

"Is she dying?" Tamara asked quietly.

"Yes," answered Chesten. "There's nothing more we can do. Whatever is causing the problems around Porthenby has been too great for her to overcome."

"Or maybe she's too old to cope any longer," Jack offered.

Tamara looked down at the sea level and felt a surge of panic at the height it had reached. Surely it must be time for the slack tide. Looking at her watch she calculated there was another hour left before the tide turned, which was worrying. "Where's the boat!" Tamara screamed.

Jack jumped up and peered over the ledge to where *Pheebz* had been secured, she wasn't there. Instinctively he looked towards the entrance and saw her being slammed and crashed against the jagged rocks surrounding the narrow exit. Watching with bated breath, as the boat was caught up in a rip current and propelled out of the cave into the open sea, he hoped she was undamaged. He realised the irony of his thought, why should he worry about a boat when maybe their lives and the Dragon's life could end this day, in this cave?

Jack turned to Chesten who dipped her head to hide her mortification — it had been one means of escape from the cave that had been yanked away from them. It had been her secret backup plan, now they were totally reliant on the lifeguards to save them. She couldn't believe her beloved old boat had abandoned them in the cave. She hoped her mother read the note soon.

A Kind Deed

Not again, thought Rupert as the mine was plunged into darkness. His unit quickly switched their torches back on and the area became flooded with welcoming light.

"Anna!" screamed Eleanor. "Where are you?"

"I'm here. Everything is fine," soothed Anna, as she grasped her sister's hand.

Did the piskie really think it would be that easy this time? thought Sam. He had caught sight of the piskie scuttling away when the torchlights flashed on. It wasn't a surprise to see him again, he had been expecting it. He looked meaner and more dishevelled since their last encounter. Anna followed his gaze and located the piskie. *Someone else can see him*, she thought. *He's not in my imagination.* Realising his discovery, he tried to blend into the dark shadows of the walls, but he couldn't hide from Anna.

"He's there, Anna," whispered Eleanor.

"I know… I've seen him."

"What should we do?" queried Eleanor. "I don't think he means harm. He's changing."

"I think the same."

"That's because you're so close to the sea Anna, it has empowered you. You are a sea goddess, the ancient Celtic Goddess, Domnu: the deity of deep water and earth," Eleanor stated in her usual off the wall manner. Thankfully, it was said in a tranquil way, which reassured Anna that her sister was fine.

"I wouldn't go that far," chuckled Anna. "I'm going to see what I can do. You'll be fine with Rupert and Kate."

"I know I'll be fine, please take care."

"I need to sort out this piskie," Anna whispered to Sam. "Keep an eye on Eleanor," she added, as she walked over to the darkness, away from the light.

No one but Eleanor and Sam noticed Anna slip away from the group. They were far too busy contacting headquarters and sorting out the exit strategy to pay her any attention. As Anna gently held out her hand to the piskie he looked perplexed, meeting the gesture with hesitation. He wondered when he had last been acknowledged warmly. *A long, long time ago,* he thought. Like a wild animal he sniffed at the hand and inhaled the ease and kindness wafting towards him. He warmed to the sensation, relaxing, eventually reaching out to grasp the offered gift. *One small kind deed can have a huge impact*, thought Anna.

He followed her meekly, away from the group... towards the exit. Leaving behind the light, security and familiarity, she entered darkness, uncertainty and the unknown. She wasn't afraid, the piskie meant her no harm, they would leave the mine together. He took the lead as the light faded and his confidence with the strange person grew. They didn't talk but walked together in a comfortable silence, as he led her around treacherous rocks and jagged edges that she was unable to see. It was like a game played amongst young children, where one child closes their eyes and puts complete trust in their friend to lead them across a hazardous path. She had played this game often with her sister, it felt familiar. Time appeared to speed up, and before long she felt the strenuous climb of the steep incline that led from the depths of the seabed to the sweet-smelling air of Botack

Headland.

Light was flooding in through the mouth of the tin mine, beckoning the pair to venture out, to wake up and leave the nightmare behind. The sound of voices, travelling from the entrance, poured into the mine and flashlights were shone in their direction causing waves of light to wash over Anna's face.

"Someone's there! Someone's coming out!" shouted one of the technicians.

"You will need to move quickly and hide yourself when we reach the exit. Others will be there," she informed her new friend. "The people will be preoccupied with me because they will want more information on what's happening in the mine. No one will see you as they aren't looking for you. In order to maintain your secrecy, you must make yourself invisible. It's easy to do, when people aren't interested in you."

It was the first time she had spoken to him, and he already knew all of what she said without being told. He was surprised that she understood the need to keep the tribe's secrecy about their existence. Maybe it was because she had spent her life protecting her sister from the painful scrutiny of unkind people. He looked at her quizzically: she was a strange person. Why was she helping him? Maybe they did have something in common? His mind cleared, and at that moment he realised he would be accepted by the elders; his time in the mine had come to an end. He didn't have the words to thank her, so he squeezed her hand tightly before disappearing into the long, wild grass of the headland.

It could have been her imagination, but Anna thought she saw a small group of piskies waiting there to welcome him back into the tribe.

A Surprise

Witnessing *Pheebz* being torn away from the cave was soul destroying for Chesten. She was unable to shake the dark clouds from her mind. Despondency settled upon her. Over and over, she kept replaying the scene, hoping to change the action, but it had been firmly set: one means of escape from this nightmare predicament she had placed them all in had been snatched away. She had taken comfort from the boat's presence, knowing she could try and steer her out of the cave if the lifeguards were unable to gain access. However, that option was no longer viable. By replaying the scene, she hoped that an alternative exit from the cave would be presented to her, but that didn't happen. She kept the thoughts to herself.

Chesten turned and watched helplessly as the Dragon struggled to lift her heavy body from her crouched position. Slowly she reared up onto her hind legs and grasped hold of a small ridge of rock a few metres above them. She gently nuzzled the rock and then fell back exhausted onto the ledge. Looking directly at Chesten, she turned and directed the girl's gaze towards the entrance of the cave. She wondered what the Dragon had seen, the seascape appeared unchanged, which was the immense ocean curling around the world and tumbling onto the shores of America.

With hardly a ripple of disturbance, the Dragon entered the ocean and fought her way out of the cave, struggling against the flood tide and rip currents. Chesten wondered why she had taken such action. If she had waited until the ebb tide, the waters would have carried her safely out through the entrance of the cave. Tamara stood beside her sister, and they stared anxiously while the Dragon determinedly cleared the entrance and swam slowly out into the vast ocean. They watched until the Dragon broke free of the rip currents and was embraced by the galloping waves.

"Ches, look here!" shouted Jack. He had scrambled up to the rocky ridge, curious to see what the Dragon had been doing. In his hand he gently held a large oval shaped egg. "There's two," he added, holding one of the eggs so the girls could see. "About the size of rugby balls."

"Be careful!" yelled Chesten, her heart racing as Jack balanced precariously on a small, narrow ledge. If he slipped and fell, the icy waters would drink him up insatiably.

"Come down, Jack," beseeched Tamara.

"I'm OK, I won't fall. There's a hot spot here, the ledge is warm and so are the eggs."

"The Dragon must have been turning the eggs," mused Chesten.

"Some kind of nest here as well. My dad said there were underground hot water springs around this area, so that's why there's a hot spot."

"Where she chose to lay her eggs," added Chesten. "Come down Jack, It's not safe balancing up there."

"They're pipping away at their shells. With this amount of activity, I reckon they'll hatch in a couple of days. When I put them close together, they squeak to each other, listen." Jack held both eggs, one in each hand. As he brought the eggs together the girls could hear the squeaks of new life surging from them, when he held them apart, they grew quieter. "They don't like being separated," Jack laughed. He carefully laid the eggs back in their nest and scrambled down.

"They must be the Dragon's eggs!" exclaimed Chesten.

"They must be! I've never seen any eggs that size before," Jack said.

"What a find! Imagine if they both hatch and we have two baby Dragons!" screeched Tamara.

A rogue wave hit the back wall, spraying the high ledge with sea water, reminding them of their situation. All thoughts of the Dragon were superseded by the threat of imminent danger. The incoming tide was too high.

"It's getting too close... the tide's higher than it should be," Chesten said quietly. "The lifeguards should be here at any moment; I'm sure mum must have read my note by now." Doubts were creeping into her mind. She knew her mum wouldn't have finished in her workshop at this time it would be at least another hour, so she wouldn't have read the note yet. She couldn't tell her little sister that. She didn't know what to do.

One Good Deed Deserves Another

After being welcomed back into the tribe, and enjoying the company of his fellow piskies, he was brought up to date with the latest news around the area. When he heard about the youngsters who had entered Mermaid Cave, the piskie hastily made his way over to Cove Cottage. He had gleaned all the information he needed from the tribe and had formed a plan; it might work.

A couple of curious adolescent piskies who had been noseying around Cove Cottage this morning, had enlightened him about the girls' movements. They said that the girls had sneaked away from home as soon as their mother had entered her workshop. The leader had left a note explaining where they were going, but she knew it wouldn't be read until later. The curious couple had laughed when they read it. Silly girl, didn't she know that by the time her mother read the note it would be too late. The tide would have swept them off the ledge and into their watery graves long before their mother had any chance to read the note. The girl hadn't been around long enough to understand the movements of the seas. It would stretch its icy fingers up and over the ledge and drag the trio into the waiting waters. Of course, the Dragon understood the tides. Her eggs were safe, just a couple of metres higher — tucked away on the short, narrow ledge that could only offer refuge to a small package. The young piskies giggled, why did adolescents think they knew all the answers? They looked slightly embarrassed as they realised the irony of their statement.

The errant piskie had been perturbed when he heard about the note. The curious couple should have told him sooner, someone should have been told, then this situation would have been resolved. He couldn't be too annoyed with their behaviour; he would have done the same… barely a few hours ago. Now it all seemed too juvenile and dangerous, peoples' lives were at risk. He was on borrowed time, he had to act swiftly. The Pascoe and Treen family had suffered enough with the passing of Tom. He needed to try and put this wrong right. It had been the troublesome threesome who had caused the fatal accident where Tom's life was wrenched away from him, but it wasn't the time for these young people to pass. He would try everything possible to prevent it. The strange person called Anna had helped him, now it was his turn to help her friends.

Peering in through the window he found Edith in her workshop, glazing the day's products. Blending in perfectly with the wisteria, which drooped languidly in the warm, still afternoon air, the piskie observed her neat, efficient movements. Her deepening frown, as she concentrated on her work, demonstrated a certain amount of stress was already present in her psyche. He could worry away at this weakness; it was a good opening for his piskie magic. It shouldn't be too difficult, she was an honest, open person. Oblivious to the imminent danger her daughters were facing, the piskie needed to draw her attention away from her work and direct it to where it was needed, the rescue of her daughters. Of course, the young lad would benefit as well, which was an added bonus, but he wasn't the main concern. He got to work immediately.

Feeling a sudden, sharp stab of pain behind her eyes,

her vision became blurred with zig zag lines travelling around her peripheral vision. Edith hadn't suffered with a migraine in years. If she acted quickly she could prevent it developing. Carefully putting the earthenware bowl onto her workbench and walking over to the kitchen to take her tablets, Edith knew the migraine would soon be dispelled. Within ten minutes she would be free of this inconvenience. The medication would work like a Trojan and drive away the unwanted symptoms. As a treat she might even have a cup of tea and a scone, which would definitely make her feel better.

Rummaging through the kitchen drawer proved fruitless; the tablets had disappeared. They were always there. *It must be the pesky piskies*, she thought angrily. *Where could they have put them?* Willing her onwards in the search, the piskie felt frustrated. Her actions were too slow — she needed to move faster. The zig zag lines grew more prominent and the vision in her left eye became tunnelled. Her migraines had never been this severe, more of an inconvenience rather than painful or debilitating. Eventually, after what seemed like an eternity to the piskie, Edith plodded upstairs towards her bedroom. An idea had drifted into her mind, as if someone had planted it there, the tablets might be in her bedside drawer. As the door swung open the first thing Edith noticed was the note on her bed. She wondered when it had been put there. Curiously, she picked up the note. Although she knew reading it would be impossible, until the migraine had cleared, she nevertheless tried. Like a puff of smoke disappearing into thin air her migraine vanished as soon as she read the first word. She never got around to taking the medication; it wasn't necessary. Satisfied, the piskie sloped off into the surrounding countryside, pleased with the outcome.

Now Edith moved swiftly... she realised her daughters' lives were in danger. Urgently, she phoned the lifeguards, who went into action immediately. Hastily, she phoned Molly and told her where their children were. Frustratedly, she tried again and again to contact Sam but was met with an unwanted unobtainable tone. Although this was expected, she cried with frustration. As panic surged through her body, she quickly phoned Harry Dyer and explained the situation in rushed, distraught, short statements. He had said not to worry about Sam; he would contact him. As he slipped his coat on, he knew that if Sam and Jasper were on their way home they would be taking the coastal path from the headland. It held the most spectacular views, which both men would appreciate. On her way to the harbour, she rang her mother and sobbed into the phone as she relayed her daughters' actions.

From three different directions, the women converged together onto Porthenby harbour, waiting for their daughters, granddaughters and son. They needed to be there when their children were rescued. They needed to be there to love them and scold them for their silly actions. They needed to be there to comfort each other.

Young Michael

Young Michael had done well. His father was proud of him. He had made a name for himself in the local vicinity. He had gained his law degree and been offered a partnership in a well-established law firm in Truro. Although he had travelled to London when attended university and enjoyed his student days there, Michael knew it was inevitable he would return to Cornwall to practise law. He couldn't settle anywhere else, the sea was in his blood, and he needed to be surrounded by it.

It was after lunch when Michael received the phone call from the lifeboat station at Porthenby. He was needed immediately; three youngsters had entered a sea cave and were in danger of being cut off by the incoming tide. Keeping his spare clothes in the boot of his car he set off towards Porthenby, after he had given a hurried report to his staff in the office who were familiar with such incidents and understood the urgency. Thinking about the tides and caves around the area he was already trying to formulate a plan of action, but he needed more details.

Becoming a volunteer member of the local lifeboat crew allowed him the much-needed spark in his life that the sea offered. He had plunged into the basic training and been accepted at the Royal National Lifeboat Institution at Poole. He had passed with flying colours and was accepted as a member of the lifeboat crew. Immersed amongst sea loving people, boats, Cornish legends and saturated with the energy of the sea was where he felt most at home: where he wanted to be.

His father was proud of him.

Pulling into the lifeboat station, he rushed in to join the crew. The boat was being launched, and he quickly changed his clothes to unite with them. The transformation was complete, he became: rescuer, hero, braveheart. His blood quickened as he felt the tingling sensation of life flowing through his veins, it felt good. As the boat plunged enthusiastically into the sea Michael was informed of the situation.

His colleagues told him three adolescents were trapped in Mermaid Cave and the flood tide would cut them off from rescue within minutes. He heard the names Jack, Tamara and Chesten being shouted above the roaring waves, they were local kids and knew the dangers of entering the cave. Several of the crew voiced their concern, wondering why the teenagers had been so reckless.

"Chesten?" queried Michael.

"Yes," was the reply he received. "Sam and Edith Pascoe's daughter."

Michael's stomach heaved when he heard that Chesten's life was in danger; his old mentor Tom Treen's granddaughter. He had often seen her with Tom, working on the boat, fishing with her grandad. *Pheebz* the boat was called; named after Tom's wife. After Tom's untimely death he had offered to buy her, but Phoebe had refused saying her granddaughter would never forgive her if she let her go. Michael had come up with another suggestion. He would look after the boat in the boatyard at Sennen Cove and keep her in good condition, until Chesten was able to take over the responsibility of her. It would be no hardship for him, and it would be a small payment for all the kind deeds Tom had done for him in the past. Phoebe had agreed to his generous offer and, over the past four years, he had enjoyed maintaining the boat — keeping her shipshape. Earlier this year, Edith had driven over to his office in Truro to ask him if he would steer the boat to Porthenby because Chesten was eager to spend time doing minor repairs and maintenance herself. He had willingly agreed to the task, saying he would enjoy taking the old boat out on the sea. He knew Chesten would want the boat nearer home; she was Tom's granddaughter.

A couple of weeks ago he had steered *Pheebz* over to Porthenby harbour and moored her there. He remembered Chesten had hardly been able to contain herself when she had seen the boat approaching the harbour. After he had passed the keys over to Phoebe, she thanked him for taking care of their precious old boat and handed the keys straight over to Chesten, saying the boat belonged to her. The young girl had jumped up and down with excitement, throwing her arms around her grandmother and thanking her over and over. Then she walked over to Michael and gave him a hug, thanking him for keeping the boat shipshape. He told her that it had been a pleasure, and reminded her that she would need an experienced sailor onboard with her if she was planning to take the boat out on the open sea. Chesten promised she would. He knew she was a sensible girl; she wouldn't take any risks.

"I know Chesten. She's Tom's granddaughter," stated Michael.

A few of the crew members nodded. They wondered what had possessed the girl to enter the cave.

We Need A Plan

Anna was waiting anxiously for the team at the entrance of the mine, she could hear their voices as they grew nearer and was relieved to see them. Eleanor ran over to her and asked if she was alright, which was the first time in her life she had ever asked that question. Sam joined them, saying he had smoothed things over with Rupert, who had been hopping mad at her disappearance but had simmered down after he had been informed about the piskie. No one in the unit queried the strange disappearance of Anna when Rupert had stated she had gone on ahead. They knew better than to rile the old man.

Rupert was pleased he had led the team out of the mine without any further complications. He had been anxious to reach the entrance and find Anna — he wouldn't rest until he knew she was safe. He waved to Anna in acknowledgment, then motioned for Jasper and Sam to follow him to the marquee, his headquarters. He told Kate and Evan to join them, knowing Bridget and Phil would already be there, keeping things running smoothly. Sam and Jasper took their phones out of their pockets and were about to turn them on. Kate and Evan knew better.

"Put them down lads. We have work to do, which is more important than what you fancy for tea tonight," Rupert commanded.

Both men put their phones down, there wasn't any signal here anyway.

"We need to act quickly and move the consignment. Did you notice the state of the walls as we walked out of the mine?" Rupert asked as he marched into the headquarters, sitting down at his desk.

"Yes Sir," replied Kate.

Both Sam and Jasper had noticed the deterioration as they had progressed through the tunnels to the exit. It was sudden and unexpected. As the piskie had withdrawn from the mine, the structure had started to crumble and decay, as if a hundred years of neglect was visited on the site in a matter of hours. Far from causing devastation in the tin mine the piskie had maintained the fabric of the place, probably in the notion of saving himself from the persistent demands of the ocean, which was constantly pleading entrance.

Kate's sharp reply and Evan's confirmation meant they were agreed, the mine was collapsing.

"We need a plan of action, one that starts today, we can't afford to wait around!" Rupert exclaimed. He motioned for his elite team to take their seats. Bridget called for refreshments; they were all fatigued, mentally and physically. Rupert was adamant they would stay until they had sorted this mess.

"We could seal up the area again," suggested Phil. Make sure it's safe and secure. Pour tons of reinforced concrete in and seal it forever — it was how the contaminated livestock was disposed of after the Chernobyl disaster."

Kate approved of the suggestion.

"If we follow that course of action the problem will be passed on to the next generation or the one after that," Bridget interrupted. "We are witnessing the devastating effects of a decision made just over a hundred years ago. One which was taken in good faith at the time. We need something more permanent. We need to rid ourselves of it … forever."

"I agree," added Evan. "If we got mechanical devices in to move the tanks it would be less dangerous than men entering the mine again."

"I'm not sure it would work," Rupert sighed. "You saw the state of the tanks. They might disintegrate if we moved them."

"What about pumping them out!" exclaimed Sam.

"Yes!" shouted Jasper. "That was suggested years ago with the oil disaster. The locals suggested the wrecked tanker could be pumped out by trawlers, but the higher officials said it was too dangerous."

"My grandad told me about it," added Rupert. "At the time there was a small window of opportunity, weather wise, to complete the pumping out. The sailors would have been safe, unfortunately the authorities didn't move fast enough. By the time they came around to the idea it was too late. Too many people making decisions and too much red tape."

"We have precious little time to complete this task before the tin mine collapses and we can't gain entry," added Jasper. Looking Rupert in the eye he continued, "Should we go with this plan?" He had no doubt who would be entering the mine to carry out this procedure: they were seated in the marquee.

It was all decided and action was taken within the hour. Rupert left the organisation of lorries and containers with specialised pumping equipment in the capable hands of Bridget and Phil. Vacuums would be created in the containers, and the gas would be safely pumped out of the tanks, travel through the pipework and into the waiting containers situated on Botack Headland. They would deal with the disposal of the gas at a later date. All that was needed, at the moment, was a safe, secure place to hold the containers full of the deadly gas.

The Best Sailor In The World

Chesten watched horrified as the waves rushed up the walls to meet them. They pounded and crashed against the sides of the cave, the sea spray saturating the air, and dampening her hair, clothes and spirit. Taking deep breaths, she tried to stem the rising panic which was flooding her body. She froze on the spot, gazing out towards the ocean, her eye transfixed on the horizon.

"What are we going to do, Ches?" Tamara whimpered. Her words didn't have any effect on her sister, who continued staring seawards, focussing on some far-reaching point in the distance. She appeared to be in a trance-like state, unable to hear her sister's pleas.

Jack reached over and held Tamara closely, "Don't cry Tammy, we'll think of something." She clung to him tightly, sobbing on his shoulder.

Chesten was aware of the mouth of the cave shrinking into insignificance, the sea was making the escape route smaller and smaller. *What escape route?* thought Chesten bitterly. The jaws were closing, they would be gobbled up. A quiet lull entered the cave as the tide began to calm. *It's not time for the slack tide,* she thought, quickly checking her watch. *What was happening?* From the corner of her eye, she saw a flash of gold catch the sunlight and reflect into the cave. The mirrored light danced around the granite walls, bobbing up and down as if it was bowing to its audience: applause please!

Turning towards the source of the flashing light, she

saw a small blue boat navigating its way towards them. A determined wooden fishing boat, speedily approaching the cave. She knew the way. She had an unusual way of moving through the water as if she was unaffected by the turmoil of the sea, cutting a straight, steady line through seemingly inconsequential water. Gold paint outlined the lettering on the bow, which glittered and winked, signalling her arrival as she appeared to aquaplane across the water. Gradually, as she drew closer, the writing became visible — it was *Pheebz*. Sadly, Chesten noticed a slight lilting towards starboard — the boat was damaged.

Skilfully navigating, with the flood tide in his favour, was the only person who could possibly manoeuvre the boat with such expertise — her grandad. She would recognise his stance anywhere. As bright as copper, his hair caught the light of the day and burnished in a halo effect around his head. He stood tall and proud at the helm and waved to her with his strong seaman's arms. He was coming to save them.

"Come on Tammy. We're getting out of here!" Chesten shouted frantically. She grabbed hold of Jack and planted a kiss on his forehead. "We're going home. Keep hold of Tamara while I help grandad."

Jack looked confused at Chesten, "What did you say?" At that moment he looked towards the mouth of the cave and saw her — *Pheebz,* drifting back into the cave on the unusually tranquil flood tide. A faint glimmer of hope slowly surfaced in Jack as he realised there might be a possibility of escape.

Chesten was busy, leaning over the side of the ledge, reaching out, trying to secure the boat. Jack hastily let go of Tamara and grabbed hold of Chesten, steadying her, allowing her to reach further. If she could secure the boat, there was a possibility Chesten would be able to navigate out of here.

"No, stay with Tamara. I can do this," Chesten insisted.

He didn't let go of her; she was too precious. Watching as she expertly secured the boat, she motioned for Jack to help Tamara embark. Knowing her sister was terrified, Tamara would need pacifying before she stepped foot onto the old boat, yet it was the offer of a way out, and they needed to act quickly. Jack held Tamara gently and guided her onto the fishing vessel. She closed her eyes tightly, putting complete faith in Jack's ability to help her board. If she couldn't see the danger, it wasn't there. He jumped aboard as soon as Tamara had embarked and held his hand out for Chesten to join him.

"We could stay in the boat until the lifeguards get here!" Jack exclaimed.

Chesten shook her head, "The boat is taking on water, she's sinking. She'll make it home, but there isn't any time to waste."

Tom smiled at Chesten and beckoned her on board, "Come on Ches, get a move on! We need to get this boat home; she needs a plaster on her wound."

Chesten responded to her grandad's command by leaping aboard and grabbing his hand to steady herself. Leaning into his strong frame she perceived the warmth of the sunshine and the smell of the sea that always followed him around. He put his arms around her, nuzzling her face with his scratchy whiskers. Chesten laughed out loud, she had missed him so much.

"We have to get out of this cave before our exit is blocked by a watery door," Tom whispered. He knew how to soothe an anxious state and kept his voice low and quiet, like the soft ripples of water on a sheltered rock pool. He understood that his granddaughter was like him;

she could keep a cool head in dangerous circumstances. She was a capable girl, the apple of his eye. Chesten stood back to give him more room to steer the boat, but Tom shook his head. He smiled encouragingly at his granddaughter. "You can do this Ches. I'll be right here at your side giving you all the instructions you need."

Chesten looked behind her at Jack and Tamara, he was managing to mollify her sister by talking to her in his soft, pacifying voice. She loved them both.

"Don't worry about them," Tom added. "As soon as we are free of this cave, they will be fine. You and *Pheebz* have a job to do."

Chesten started the engine, which she though was strange because she couldn't remember her grandad switching it off. Cautiously she eased the boat around and headed for the exit. It was a tiny space to steer through, with jagged rocks lining the path. *I can do this*, she thought. For some reason the tide had turned earlier than its allocated time, and she surmised that it was the period of calm before the ebb tide. Maybe she had calculated the tide times incorrectly, she didn't think so. She concentrated and listened carefully while her grandad clearly and serenely gave her instructions in his old familiar way. She followed them to the letter. She wasn't afraid, not with him by her side guiding the way.

"Grandad, why has the slack tide arrived early?" asked Chesten, as she fell into the familiar routine of steering the old fishing vessel.

"You'll see, Ches. When we exit the cave." He was playing his old tricks, rather than give a direct reply he liked to lead her towards the answer. He reasoned it made her think clearer. Chesten grinned at him, she recognised the game.

Navigating through the entrance was a tight squeeze.

Pheebz's memory of the journey served her well, allowing her to avoid jagged rocks and a tricky rip current that would have sent them hurtling back into the cave, to a certain death. Tamara had her eyes firmly closed and clung petrified onto Jack. He longed to be at Chesten's side but was unable to leave Tamara, she needed him.

As the boat hit the open sea, the afternoon sun swam all around them, it was a gentle awakening from the terrifying nightmare. Tamara felt the change in the sea's movements as the boat began swaying gently. Opening her eyes, she cheered when she realised they had escaped the horrors of the watery tomb. Chesten was at the helm, her wild hair alive with the wind and sea spray. It was curling and dancing around her head, a sight that never failed to please Tamara. She squinted, aiming to get a clearer look: something was different. Her hair seemed darker than its usual shade, with threads of steely grey woven throughout. It reminded her of someone else; someone older. She blinked hard and looked again. Remarkably, Chesten's hair had resumed its former glory. Tamara held the previous image in her mind, it was surreal.

"Jack, Tamara, look... over there!" shouted Chesten, pointing dead ahead. It was a sad sight. The Dragon had made herself into a massive breakwater, in an attempt to calm the flood tide that tore its way into the cave. The heavy Atlantic waves pounded her frail body, which was breaking under the strain. She was tossed and rolled in the churning waters and struggled to maintain her position. Her body divided and disintegrated, mixing with the chaotic ocean currents: at last finding peace. The myriad of colours dispersed amongst the frothy waters and lost all shape and form. Within minutes the Dragon had disappeared from sight, as though she had never existed.

"She saved us!" cried Tamara.

Lorries with specialist pumping equipment were on site within the hour. Reinforced concrete arrived in transit mixers and the place was a hive of activity. The speed of the response impressed Sam and Jasper. It was what Rupert expected from Bridget and Phil, they made a good team and worked well together.

As Sam and Jasper prepared themselves for re-entry into the mine, Rupert suggested a message should be sent to Edith and Molly who would be expecting their men back any time soon and would be worried if they didn't appear. Sending a simple message, stating they were sorting logistics out with Rupert would save their wives from worrying. Bridget was on the case immediately and used the landline to contact the police station at Porthenby — they would convey the message. Landlines were far more reliable in Cornwall, with its notoriously poor mobile phone reception. Meanwhile Phil had arranged for an ambulance and medical team to be on standby at the headland. The operation was becoming more dangerous as the day progressed, and it might be needed. He hoped not. Sam struggled with not allowing himself to think about the perils of the mission. He would set his mind to the task and deal with whatever happened. Jasper thought about his boy. He hoped his son would never undertake such a dangerous mission. He was sure he wouldn't; Jack was too sensible.

Rupert led his team back into the mine, followed by his specialist unit armed with equipment to attach to the tanks in preparation for the pumping out. The lights had been fixed, and the team made good progress towards the sealed off chamber. They tried not to focus on the crumbling walls and seeping water as they made their journey through the mine. There was no point in dwelling on it, the job had to be done.

The heavy metal door reluctantly creaked open, jamming on concrete rubble strewn in its path; it resented further intrusion. Like uninvited guests, the team entered the chamber, oblivious of the annoyance their interference caused. Within minutes an adequate lighting system was fixed, which would help ensure the smooth running of the operation. The chamber was blinded by the harsh brightness and strenuously tried to adjust to the violation. It had been promised peace and sanctuary but what were the words of men?

Sam and Jasper set about helping the specialist unit attach the pipes to each of the six tanks, and time gradually woke up and began to move forwards. The chamber had maintained this space-time for over a hundred years and began to mourn its passing as seconds and minutes fought their way back into existence. The preserved chamber prepared itself for the operation; everything was about to change.

The team's concentration was focused on completing the task; nothing else. The specialists ran the pipes from the tanks and fed them through the mine, towards the exit. When they reached the headland, the pumping out would begin.

"Time for you to go now boys," Rupert said quietly but firmly, when the last tank had been prepared for pumping out.

"What will you be doing?" asked Sam.

"I'll be staying to make sure the attachments hold and the pumping is completed," replied Rupert.

"Then that's what I'll be doing," replied Sam.

"Me too," added Jasper.

Rupert sighed, there was no point arguing with them, they were both as stubborn as mules.

"OK," he announced. "However, if I say we go… we go. Whatever we're doing we down tools and go." The matter was settled, Sam and Jasper would stay.

A deep rumbling and dragging noise could be heard as the pipes that would deliver the concrete into the storage area were being laid along the floor of the mine. The sound reverberated throughout the mine, causing the deteriorating walls and roof to release more crumbling concrete. It fell in chunks, particles and powder, surrounding the men, reducing their visibility. Sam looked around and was reminded of Cove Cottage, once upon a time, long ago, covered in freshly fallen snow. A rare occurrence in Cornwall. Tamara had said their home looked like a cottage in a fairy tale and ran to find a pencil and paper, she needed to draw. Centre stage stood Cove Cottage, small and frail, covered with snow and surrounded by woodland, not its usual setting of fields, sand and sea. With concentration, and a vivid imagination, a dragon could be seen woven throughout the trees, becoming part of the woodland. It completely encircled the cottage, providing strength and protection. Sam had wondered where she had got the idea from. At eight-year-old she had won first prize at the local art show with her drawing. Her talent was obvious, even at such a young age. The memory filled him with longing, he hoped he would see his family and home again.

Via the walkie talkie system Rupert instigated the

signal. The pumping out from the headland began. It was a quiet whirring noise that swirled around the tanks as the gas was sucked out of them. Jasper envisioned the sleeping, lethal gas waking up, understanding that it was time to go.

Did it hear the three blasts of the whistle? Was it time to go over the top? Did it think it would be released and allowed to cause havoc and death? The very purpose of its existence. Or was it a thoughtless creature that moved around wherever it was instructed to go?

Jasper could sense the gas travelling along the pipes and into the waiting containers. An old enemy, tired and worn out but still deadly; there wasn't any room for mistakes to be made. Everything was going to plan. Jasper wondered how long it would take.

Rupert acknowledged that the piping for the concrete had reached the chamber and released the technicians from their duties, it would be six less people who were in this precarious situation. Six less people whose safety and lives he was responsible for. One stubborn lad, Ethan, refused to leave explaining he had expertise in this area and was needed. Reluctantly Rupert agreed; he knew the lad was right.

"And then there were four," Rupert muttered.

The waiting was tortuous as the gas made its way along the pipework, seeking its new home. Unsuspectingly it travelled towards an empty vacuum, not the rolling fields and woodlands that it had been promised. The atmosphere in the mine was too tense for small talk, with every member constantly checking the tanks for leakage and ensuring the gas was still flowing. Rupert had positioned Kate and Evan on the headland, their orders were clear — to make sure everything was progressing safely at their end. His last orders were that on no account should they enter the mine.

Eventually, the first tank emptied, and the gas was transported to the old RAF site. The whole consignment would be stored there until a permanent solution of its disposal could be found. Rupert let out a sigh of relief: things were going to plan. Ethan started manoeuvring the pipework, for the delivery of the concrete, through a hole he had cut into the wall of the chamber. The feeder pipe was set higher than the tanks, so they would become totally immersed in concrete. Rupert considered it to be a necessary precaution, it would secure and make safe any residual gas that may be left in the tanks. Rupert was pleased the lad had stayed, they wouldn't have been able to complete the task as quickly and efficiently without him.

Ethan explained that when the pipework and pumping out was completed all the tools would be left behind in the chamber, they would need to make a quick exit without being hindered by any surplus weight. Rupert agreed, he imagined the tanks drowning in the suffocating, cloying material which would quickly set and constrict them: crushing the remains of any menace left behind. As the last tank emptied Ethan gave a thumbs up sign, and Rupert contacted the headland sanctioning the release of the concrete into the storage area. It would be tricky; the concrete had a long way to travel. Rupert had every confidence that the calculations of the factors to ensure the concrete would travel the distance would be correct, but he still crossed his fingers as it rumbled through the pipework and fell into the chamber.

"OK lads. Time for us to go."

As they sealed the door behind them, they heard the concrete slushing against the walls and door, slowly but surely filling the storage area. The team hastily followed Rupert, as he led the way out of the mine, along the rapidly decaying passageway. A growing feeling of triumph was settling in Rupert's stomach as they neared the exit; a job well done. They saw a pinhole of daylight which meant freedom, it was within easy grasp. He turned to face his two friends and grinned.

"We've done it!" cheered Sam.

Sam's cheering was met with a loud horrendous crashing and breaking racket. The roof was falling. It wasn't in a rush; it took a leisurely pace. Parodying slow motion, it arranged debris chaotically in front of the men. Freedom was being denied. Rupert shouted out in pain. His right leg was trapped under blocks of ancient, gnarled concrete. Like a moth pinned lifeless onto a board. The team jumped back shocked and dazed.

"Is everyone OK?" shouted Jasper. Dust and mud flew in every direction, choking and blinding the team, wrenching hope of safety from them. The lights were ripped out plunging the mine, yet again, into the thick, cloying blackness of a nightmare. Unfortunately, the LED torches had been left behind with the rest of their heavy equipment. Jasper felt in his pocket for his talisman, his old torch. He carried it everywhere.

"I'm trapped!" yelled Rupert.

Sam was on his hands and knees in an instant crawling along the floor, searching for Rupert. Their exit was barred by the downfall of rubble and timbers. He needed to find his friend as quickly as possible and exit the mine, or be entombed there… forever. Old timbers creaked and groaned with the weight of centuries of displeasure brought about by granite and minerals being prevented from following their natural course, into the mine. The mine meant them no harm, but the waiting had been too long. The inevitability of the movement of land was overdue. When something is denied, it becomes all the more desired.

From the tone of his friend's voice, Sam knew that Rupert was in pain. The slimy seawater, polluted with concrete dust, froze his fingertips as he groped around in the darkness. Gradually, the dust began to settle, and the torch beam feebly forced its way through the dust and debris, enabling Sam to see the outline of Rupert's body squashed against the floor. He was trapped; the mine held him prisoner. Throwing chunks of debris in all directions, Sam desperately tried to free his friend.

"STOP!" shouted Ethan.

Jasper put his hand on Sam's shoulder, halting his movements. A low creaking and breaking sound, of timbers fracturing and breaking free from their ties, thundered through the walls. The mine was starting to fall in on itself.

"We need to work carefully," explained Ethan. "If we pull those slabs away the whole wall could collapse on us. I know it's difficult, but we have to work slower. We can free Rupert if we move and restack the slabs, shoring up the wall."

Jasper looked around him. He knew they were above sea level, not far from the exit, but how many tons of concrete barred their way? Even if they managed to free Rupert, would they be able to exit the mine before it collapsed? He shook the thought from his head and followed Ethan's directions, gently moving slabs of debris off Rupert and restacking them against the fragile wall. *Don't think any further than this moment in time*, he thought.

Satisfied the men were working carefully and following his instructions, Ethan studied the mountain of debris obstructing their way out. He tapped and prodded the monster until he found a weak spot in her frame.

Excitedly he told the men that they could possibly break through at that point.

Rupert was released from his captivity and was made comfortable by his friends. He could see Ethan was making good progress tunnelling into the body of the monster and told Jasper and Sam to help the lad; he was unable to.

The Warmth Of The Sunshine And Smell Of The Sea

As quick as lightning, the lifeboat raced through the tempestuous Atlantic Ocean. This was what she was built for; this was her purpose. Michael gauged the height of the flood tide; it was distressing. Suggestions and ideas were thrown around the boat. How would they rescue the youngsters? The whole crew knew, very shortly, the Mermaid Cave entrance would be blocked by the tide. Arthur, an offshore gas surveyor, was preparing his diving equipment. He intended swimming into the cave in an attempt to save the kids. Maybe he could find a ledge where they could wait safely until the ebb tide mercifully allowed access into the cave. He doubted that; it would be too late. The atmosphere on the lifeboat was thick and depressing. Yet the lifeboat still sprinted across the sea as if her own life depended upon it. It was all she could do.

The small boat bobbed up and down on the swell of the waves. Michael squinted his eyes, focussing on the fishing vessel; it was *Pheebz.* He pointed her out to the crew members who trained their binoculars on her while they counted three young people aboard. Michael could do better than that, he could verify it was Chesten, Tamara and a young lad, probably Jack. He emitted a deep sigh, and the tension was released from his body as he realised they hadn't entered the cave. He knew

Chesten was too sensible to attempt anything so reckless. Scanning over the three teenagers, making sure his observations were correct, he noticed that something was not quite right. Difficult to put into words. He thought there was a fourth person on board, someone standing beside Chesten at the helm of the boat. He recognised the figure but knew it couldn't be. Maybe it was the confident stance of the person standing at the helm, or the flash of red hair as the sunbeams bounced off it — he wasn't sure.

Arthur was also scanning the boat, "Three youngsters," he confirmed.

Michael looked again and the image faded. It was three people.

"The mother must have relayed the message incorrectly to the lifeboat station, the kids obviously haven't been in the cave: they wouldn't have been able to navigate out of there!" declared Emma, the onboard mechanic.

"Still, they need rescuing — by the way the boat is presenting herself she's damaged," added Arthur.

Jubilation swamped throughout the crew as they swung the lifeboat out to sea, towards *Pheebz.* Sea spray was churned up by the vigorous movements of the lifeboat and soared high into the air as she hurried towards the old fishing boat. Two friends rushing to meet each other.

"Is everyone OK?" Michael shouted above the constantly chattering sea, as they pulled up alongside the small boat.

"Everyone OK," yelled Jack. "And pleased to see you."

Michael helped the teenagers board the lifeboat, Tamara and Jack first. Unexpectedly, Chesten refused to leave her boat.

"Don't worry, I'll steer her home — she'll make it. I wouldn't leave her behind," he held his hand out for Chesten, but she was still hesitant.

Looking around *Pheebz* in a confused manner, a deep sadness slowly crept across her face etching lines of bewilderment and longing. Ruffling her hair and stroking her cheek the sea breeze muttered under its breath, "It's time for you to go now Ches."

Tears streamed down her face as the essence of the sunshine and the spirit of the sea drifted away leaving behind the brightness of the day and the smell of the ocean.

"Arthur, help me with this one. She's in shock."

Disobeying Orders

As Kate and Evan peered into the mine and saw the team making their way towards them, they were elated. The old man had done it and returned safely. The image disappeared in an instant. The curtain came down on the returning party. Horrified, Kate and Evan witnessed the mine collapsing, blocking the exit for Major Angove and his team. Their training took over and they immediately organised a rescue party. Kate picked up the walkie talkie and tried to contact Rupert… it was dead. Within minutes an army of people were moving debris in an effort to reach the trapped men, shoring up the sides of the mine to prevent further collapse. Knowingly acting against orders, Kate and Evan would deal with the consequences later. Kate signalled for the men to be quiet as she listened intently for any signs of life on the dark side of the barrier. The rescue team disregarded the hindering moans and groans of the mine and concentrating on finding the sound of human movement or voices.

"I can hear a tapping," announced Kate, "it's faint but definitely there."

Evan moved over towards Kate and sat quietly, waiting for his ears to pick up on the sound. It was unquestionably a digging noise; they were tunnelling out.

"Over here!" ordered Evan. "This is where we dig."

"Wouldn't be surprised if we met the old man halfway," joked Kate.

The tin mine continuously warned the rescuers of the danger they were in, bidding them to down tools and move away, with its rumbling groaning voice. The crumbling walls and exposed timbers of the mine didn't intentionally threaten their lives, it didn't intend inflicting any more pain and suffering. The mine had seen enough devastation during its long years of service. Men, women and children had worked their fingers to the bone in the hellish setting, some had lost their lives. So many sad, disillusioned, worn-out people. As the mine disintegrated, dark thoughts and memories that were buried in the wooden beams and hiding in the damp walls, were released. The mine longed for solitude, it needed freedom from human intervention. It aimed to be at one with the surrounding land. It was time to scour the fabric of the place, free it from all the suffering and unhappiness it had endured, dilute it in the vastness of the ocean. Start afresh.

Ignoring the impending danger, Kate and Evan ordered the rescue party to continue clearing the debris. It was Kate who first saw the tiny fingers of light appear from the other side of the rubble.

"Major Angove!" shouted Kate.

At the sound of Kate's voice and the glare from her flashlight, Sam felt a surge of hope trickle through his veins. He would see his family again. As the rescue party broke through into the mine, Jasper quickly informed the medics there was only one casualty — Rupert. He was badly bruised with a possible broken leg.

The medics made arrangements for Rupert to be carefully lifted into the waiting ambulance and transported from the headland to the Royal Cornwall Hospital. Jasper reassured him, saying it was merely a precaution, he needed checking over, and his leg did need medical attention.

"I will talk with Kate and Evan first," Rupert insisted.

Knowing they had disobeyed orders the two elite members of Rupert's team came forward, prepared to receive whatever consequences were dealt them. Their instincts told them their elite status was about to disappear.

"When I give an order, I expect it to be carried out… to the letter. There's no room for negotiation. Both of you disobeyed my orders. You do realise the whole of the rescue party could have been killed in the mine!"

Kate and Evan remained silent. They had expected this.

"However, I want to thank you for saving my life and also my friends' lives. I won't be taking any action against you for not following orders… this time. Make sure it doesn't happen again!"

As the ambulance set off on its journey to Truro, Sam and Jasper made their way home. They had been checked over by the medics who concurred that their injuries, cuts and bruises, were superficial. They could go home. With such poor reception in the area there was no point trying to use their mobile phones, and the landline in the marquee was busy — with Bridget consulting with the hospital about Rupert's condition.

The two friends walked back towards Porthenby via the coastal path; it was a relaxing route. They were encouraging their bodies to destress after such an eventful day. The spring sunshine warmed their chilled bodies, busy nesting birds served to recharge their energy levels, and the sheer cliffs reintroduced joy and wonder. There was a comfortable silence between the two old friends, no need for conversation. The Cornish coastline worked its magic, and they began to mellow.

"SAM! JASPER!"

Both men looked down the cliff path and saw Harry Dyer waving his arms around frantically.

"What does he want?" Sam queried, as a sickening feeling tightened his stomach.

"Don't know, but it looks urgent," replied Jasper as the two men ran down the path towards Harry.

Edith flung her arms around her daughters, sobbing and laughing at the same time. Molly hugged Jack as tightly as she could. They were safe. Sam and Jasper were intent on getting their families home, but Jack was reluctant to leave Chesten, the girl was still in shock. He held her hand, letting her know he was there, but the far-off look in her eye signalled she was in some other place; someplace he couldn't be.

Phoebe solved the dilemma, "Let's all go to Cove Cottage. I can help get some food ready, and you silly monkeys can tell us all about your adventure."

The tension eased, and everyone agreed with the suggestion; the problem was solved. Slowly the party made their way to the cottage with Tamara and Jack talking constantly about the Dragon, her eggs, and Chesten's amazing feat of navigating *Pheebz* out of Mermaid Cave.

Phoebe insisted Chesten would be fine and didn't need to be hospitalised, she simply needed rest and quiet — at home. She knew what was troubling her granddaughter. Sam and Edith agreed, thinking it would be far more beneficial for Chesten to settle down at home rather than endure the trauma of being admitted to hospital; the girl had been through enough.

Michael grinned like a Cheshire cat. The families were reunited, and no one was hurt. He wished every rescue turned out this way. The youngsters had been very quiet on the way back to the harbour, huddled together for comfort and support. Michael assumed they were embarrassed about being rescued — thinking themselves to be able seafarers. Or maybe the silence was because they had damaged the boat. He was surprised at the change in their demeanour when they had met up with their parents. Tamara and Jack had burst into non-stop chatter about the Dragon, and Chesten's amazing feat of navigating the boat out of the cave. What on earth had they been talking about? It was probably shock — he'd seen it affect people in many different ways.

Sam and Jasper stayed behind to thank Michael and the rescue crew. As for the case of the possible fourth person in the boat? Michael understood that he should keep that information to himself. Who would believe him? It was probably a trick of the light. Smoke and mirrors. Mischief and trickery.

Burning brightly, the ash logs warmed and comforted the two families as they settled into the cottage and talked about the day's events. The Dragon's death had been recounted mournfully by Tamara and Jack, and a web of sorrow was spun across the gathering. Edith said it may have been time for the Dragon to pass and no amount of help could have saved her, they would just have to wait and see what happened next. Chesten gradually became more aware of her surroundings and accepted a cup of tea from Jack, smiling at him.

"Thanks for being here," she whispered in his ear.

"I'm always here for you, Ches."

Phoebe noticed the change in her granddaughter's manner and sat down beside Chesten, understanding the girl's need to recount her ordeal. She took hold of her granddaughter's hand, "Do you want to tell me about it?"

Drawing breath, Chesten began her story. "It was so

cruel. He was there when we were out on the sea with *Pheebz*. Then he drifted away into the sunshine and sea leaving behind a space in life where he should be… but he's unable to be there. Everyone thinks it was me who navigated the boat out of the cave, but they're wrong: it was grandad. He was there guiding me. I couldn't have done it without him. Now he's gone. I miss him so much. I didn't realise how much I missed him until today. He's fading as time moves on, and I want him to stay. I need him to stay." Phoebe cradled her granddaughter in her arms, soothing away the sorrow.

"I must be going mad," sobbed Chesten. "How could grandad have been there? No one else saw him. Not Tamara, Jack or any of the lifeboat crew. What's wrong with me?"

"He will always be there for you Chesten," Phoebe murmured in her ear. "I saw him too."

Chesten looked quizzically at her grandmother, waiting for an explanation.

"He was in *Pheebz,* standing at the helm. I saw him as soon as the lifeboat turned and pulled into the harbour. He was standing tall and proud with his signature crop of red hair blazing in the Cornish sunlight. He waved to me and smiled. Such a happy smile, my heart melted. I knew at that moment he had made the journey to rescue all of you. He didn't stay for long because he couldn't. As the lifeboat entered the harbour, the sun filtered through him and the sea spray broke up the image. But it was him."

The room was silent as the conversation ended between granddaughter and grandmother. Everyone had heard.

Tamara thought back to her time on the boat, the image of another presence. "I believe you Ches. There was something different on the boat. Something that didn't make sense." Drawing in her sketch book, while conversations had been flowing around the room, Tamara showed her sister the picture. She had captured the likeness, the essence of the man. There he was, in black and white, standing beside Chesten at the helm of the boat. Chesten strong and capable. Her grandad vague and ethereal guiding her hands on the wheel: navigating them to safety.

Both families stared at the drawing.

A Triumvirate

"Eye of newt, and toe of frog,
Wool of bat, and tongue of dog,
Adder's fork, and blond-worm's sting,
Lizard's leg, and howlet's wing."

The errant piskie was huddled down in a form with a couple of hares. They observed the adolescents curiously. The group of local teenagers had made their way over onto Porthenby Island, the three adventurers who intrigued him were with them. The piskie tutted, they were messing about, chanting powerful spells. On a place such as this they were asking for trouble. *Double, double toil and trouble*, he thought, smirking to himself. They were probably voicing loose words without meaning, he'd seen kids play like this before. At least it wasn't the threesome who were chanting, now that would be interesting.

Sneaking around the Pascoe and Lee households, he had been eavesdropping on conversations and actions over the past couple of days. He was nosey and wondered how this story would pan out. There had been hours and hours of talking about the eggs. Twin Dragons might hatch, the mother had stated — well that was obvious. *Double, double,* he thought. After an eternity of talking, they had agreed to leave the eggs alone. It was about the only sensible decision they had made. He could have told them that. Then there was the matter of the toxic consignment — how was it going to be made safe? If they had left well alone the Dragon would have sorted everything; she always did. The pragmatist, Rupert he was called, had arranged for discussions and now plans were being made, yawn, yawn. At least he had the sense to include his two friends in the decision making; they were strong together. They were beginning to recognise this fact.

He was pleased the old tin mine had been sealed, immediately after its collapse. He never wanted to see the place again. The taste of freedom was good, like sweet blossom honey from the meadow bees. For over a hundred years he had been constantly fighting against the needs of the surrounding land and sea that were determined to swamp the place. He had managed to hold the mine together while he had been confined there, but once he had left the place it had heaved a great sigh of relief as it eased itself into its new desired position. It would be content now. He had no intention of being imprisoned again, he would endeavour to follow the guidance of the elders. Keep to the straight and narrow. Try to control himself…

The threesome had been let loose today, after lots of discussions, yawn, yawn, so boring, and lots of chastising. They had promised that they wouldn't do anything like that again. They didn't fool him they were too headstrong, all three of them. It was Easter Sunday, and their mothers had said they needed to meet up with their friends: it would do them good. They were contrite, all would be well, said the mothers. So, the fathers had agreed. Two days they had been confined in their homes, pondering about their actions. Two days since they had escaped the maws of the beast. Easter Sunday, the time of rebirth and new beginnings. *Interesting*, thought the piskie.

The chanters collapsed onto the springy turf, giggling and laughing.

"She's not here!" shouted one of the boys from the group, as he peered over the edge of the island into the mysteries of the sea.

The piskie turned, faced the hares and shrugged his shoulders when he realised the youngsters were trying to summon the Dragon.

The hares whispered in unison that they were looking in the wrong place. They needed to be on the bridge. Also, she would never swim in on the ebb tide, it was always on the flood tide when she appeared. The hares paused and shook their heads, saying, "But that won't happen now. She's dead." They found it hard to believe the teenagers didn't know she wasn't around anymore. The last statement shocked the piskie, he knew it was true, but hearing it from the hares reinforced the fact. He turned away from them, hiding his emotion as a tear slid down his old, wrinkled face.

She had been around forever, at least that's what the tribe had told him. The truth was nobody knew when she first appeared, but no one would admit it — the elders liked to appear all knowing. He first met her way back in time, when people lived on the island. Ah, the good old days, when life was so much simpler. He had been a youngster then and was in awe of her power. She had been widely acknowledged, respected and worshipped during those times. A fitting tribute to her achievements.

As time passed, he increasingly thought that she basked in the glory of being considered a necessary and important part of life, revelling in her role as a piece of the jigsaw. She had found a niche, made herself indispensable, and he began to find her growing ego tiring.

As he grew and began forming adult opinions their relationship drifted apart, as some friendships do, but he always expected it to return… someday. They had developed different mindsets. She could never relax and chill out; always busying around rectifying problems. She could never take a joke or laugh at a prank and increasingly his life took that line. He couldn't pander to her ego, as most creatures did, and so the gap between them grew wider and wider. For the past couple of centuries they hadn't been on good terms: she could never forgive a disloyal act dealt against her. He did try to reconnect with her when he was imprisoned in the tin mine, anything to relieve the boredom of his confinement. However, the distance between them had become insurmountable. She had ignored him.

He had always assumed she was a constant, and sometime in the future she would find it in her heart to forgive him. He didn't expect her to die. He'd seen her in similar situations, when the toils of some seemingly insurmountable problem had ravaged her body. He'd seen her in the process of dying on a few occasions, and that's what it was… a process. It was reversible and she always broke free from its clutches and renewed herself. Regenerated her body and grew stronger. Yes, he knew she was dying, but he didn't expect her to die.

The hares told him everything comes to an end; nothing stays the same forever. Actions have consequences, and the reason for the Dragon's death would soon become known. We all need to be patient, they said. They were so laid back in their approach to life they were practically horizontal. He told the hares about the poisonous gas and surmised it was the cause of her death. Unfortunately, this time the Dragon had allowed the process of death to travel too far, and it had become irreversible, past the point of no return.

"Could be," the hares had answered, again speaking in unison.

Rather a lazy way of talking, he thought. The hares asked him if he had considered it may be one generation making way for the next, allowing for change and advancement to develop without the constraints of elders stifling new ideas and creativity. Paving the way for new life, as was the natural order. The piskie looked at them quizzically, he hadn't considered that. He asked if the Dragon had confided in them. They remained silent, they were not disloyal and would not betray her. If only he could turn the clock back and keep the Dragon's confidences. He should have kept her secret; the place she visited on the ebb tide. He had only shared the secret with the hares, and they wouldn't repeat it to anyone so what was the problem? He sighed with regret.

Glancing at the adventurers, who were passing secretive, coded looks between each other, he understood they wouldn't share any knowledge of the Dragon with their friends. They would remain loyal. He realised, at that moment, that he had misread the actions of the group. They weren't summoning the Dragon they were tormenting the threesome, ridiculing and laughing at them. Young people can be so cruel. Their mothers had said this would happen. Ignore it, they said. People will forget about it in a couple of weeks.

He studied the threesome: they were supporting each other. They could endure the taunts from their peers, they could even laugh with them.

The younger sister had the making of a good storyteller, he realised. Her stories unfolded from the sketches and paintings she produced, portraying far more depth than mere words were able to conjure up. Her friends crowded around, curious to see what she had sketched from the play acting, they were surprised. She had drawn mustard seed, buttercup, holly leaves, hounds' tongue, adder's tongue and blind-worm. All the ingredients the old herbalists used when making up their concoctions. Those witches were good at keeping their potions a mysterious secret by using disturbing names, he had admired them. Smoke and mirrors.

As for the boy, well it was obvious, he had a way with animals. A whisperer, he had heard some call him. It ran in his family, and he had inherited the gene, probably from both parents. The trait was strong in him

And the older sister… she was a natural leader. People listened to her and became like-minded. She generated an aura of energy and excitement that people longed to be immersed in. Although small in stature she had the knack of persuasion; she appeared larger than her size. Smoke and mirrors. She reminded him of some queen he knew in days of yore; a Celtic queen who had fulfilled her duties wisely. She had uncomplainingly traipsed around all day after her head in the clouds husband, listening to him preaching about fairness and round tables. It was enough to drive anyone to distraction. Yet, for a short while, she had survived the ordeal, by entering a forbidden, passionate, doomed love affair. Some say she had been flawed, nevertheless in his mind that made her all the more interesting. Yes, he could see the similarities, they had the same presence, bearing and determination. She made life interesting. People believed in this older sibling. It wasn't a criticism, more of an observation.

So here it was — a triumvirate. They were innocents.

Unaware of the fact; oblivious of their joint strength. He wondered if he should leave well alone or intervene. After conferring with the elders, he agreed to abstain from any actions that may quell their potential… for the present. Maybe together they would do more good than harm. Maybe life would take them all in different directions, it often did. Then they would lose their unique power.

After sharing his thoughts with the hares, and listening to their advice, he bid them farewell and slipped out of the form, making his way back home. It was always good to have a second opinion, and the hares formed part of his significant others whose counsel he respected. They agreed with the decision of the elders and reminded him that Porthenby was settling back down onto an even keel.

The hens were laying again — about time, they were spoilt and lazy.

The scrawny pigeons had finally found their way home — they shouldn't have trusted the usurper.

He had seen a Porthenby crab in one of the more secluded rockpools — they liked to keep themselves to themselves.

The calves were getting steadier on their feet — time they did stand up for themselves, they were too well looked after.

Unfortunately, nothing could be done about the lambs — some people were unable to stop interfering with nature and this was the price to be paid.

The seals were another matter — they had swum too close to the old mine, noseying around, wondering what the Dragon had been doing. Curiosity killed the cat, or in this case, seals.

As for Edith's spoilt glazes, well, he'd grown tired of that prank. Let the woman alone was the advice offered by the elders, and he had agreed with them.

Oh well, you win some you lose some, thought the piskie. *Time to let sleeping dogs lie.*

Walking away from the island, with a small purse in his hand he had taken from one of the girls in the group, he hid it in the long grass. It wouldn't be difficult to find, but the teenagers would be flustered, and the purse would become invisible to them. He snickered at his mischief. They would spend ages looking for it. When it couldn't be found they would blame each other. He laughed out loud. Old habits die hard.

As he walked back home across the fields, towards the woods where the tribe was gathered, he thought about the task he had set for the troublesome threesome. The unruly piskies he had been mentoring. He hoped they completed their task to his exact instructions. Sometimes they had a habit of taking matters into their own hands. The elders had decided to recruit him into helping out with the role of coaching the young members, they were sure it would be beneficial for both parties. The errant piskie had eagerly accepted the role, it would earn him some credibility in the tribe.

Only a few hours ago, the curious couple had told him that they had overheard a few elders discussing his renaming ceremony. Over time piskie names inevitably change, due to events, actions and relationships forming their personalities. The names chosen reflect their psyche, and in his opinion he had been long overdue a name transition. The piskie told them that he felt sure he would be awarded a more positive moniker, something more suitable such as adventurer or wise one, which would be a sure sign that he was moving up in the tribe. The curious couple smiled and shook their heads. They said that neither of those names had been chosen.

The piskie's mind drifted and the woman called Anna was conjured up, she was engaging. It was the way she rolled with the flow of life; never trying to contain it. She wasn't fooled by the illusion of control. He had never met anyone like her in all of his life, which was very long. Serendipity — that was his plan.

Looking up into the sky, he saw the gathering of the dark clouds and felt the first fat, heavy raindrops on his weathered skin. They smelled wrong and were strangely shaped. Someone or something was orchestrating this. He had a good idea who. *Double, double,* he thought.

A Song From Long Ago

Laughing and joking, the troublesome threesome had turned around all signposts leading to Penzance. Not many people would be on time for the concert tonight! There wouldn't be much point anyway because the star of the show was driving away from his venue and heading towards Porthenby. Eventually, they diverted most of the traffic back onto the main road in a loop heading towards Penzance. Frustrated and confused when they knew they would be late for the show, arguments erupted between passengers and drivers. Some of the drivers became lost and disheartened, so they abandoned their night out and searched for the way home. The piskies were in hysterics. Even in the midst of all their frivolity they made sure that one person who was following their confusing signposts, missed the diversion back towards Penzance. They directed him towards Porthenby: it was their task.

The musician was perplexed as he drove down the road into Porthenby. He wondered how on earth he had ended up there, the very place he had tried to avoid. His sat-nav had stopped working the moment he crossed the Cornish border, which wasn't a surprise. The Cornish highways became familiar once again, as his recall of roads, lanes and tracks came flooding back. Annoyingly, some of the roads had changed, causing him to be unsure of where he was heading. He hadn't been in this part of the country for decades.

Old memories started knocking on the door and demand he pay attention to them. They disturbed him; some good, some bad. He hadn't been comfortable about accepting his manager's decision to play at the Penlee Park Open Air Theatre. For one night only, the flyer had stated. It was a sell-out. His manager predicted his show would be a success and couldn't understand his reluctance to set foot in the westerly county. After all, most of his hit recordings were about the Cornish sea and the love of his life — a sea goddess: it would appeal to the local audience. He was persuaded he could cope with one night in Cornwall and had reluctantly agreed. It had all happened a long time ago; a lifetime had passed. Maybe it was time to let go of the past, the missed adventures… and lost love. Still, the memories haunted him at times.

He needed to find his way out of this place quickly and hot foot it to Penzance, otherwise there would be a lot of disappointed fans. But first he felt the need to park his car and walk on the beach. Feel the sand beneath his feet, stretch his tired limbs, give himself some time to think. Walking along the cobbled road and onto the beach, he felt young again: each step seemed to tear away at all the years of regret and loss.

It was pure serendipity finding her there, sauntering on the beach with her younger sister at her side. She recognised him immediately and began walking towards him. She was still as beautiful as the reflection of the moon on the peaceful slack tide.

"Anna?" he said quietly, as they stood together. She smiled at him, the freckles on her face scrunching up, reminding him of the girl he loved from long, long ago.

Eleanor made her way off the beach and walked back home. Her sister needed time for herself, and that was as it should be. Those two had a lot of catching up to do. She began to experience a sense of freedom swirl around her in welcoming eddies: she had waited a long time for this. Each step loosened her bond with Anna, like a toddler's first unbalanced footsteps that enabled them to break free from the safety of their mother, preparing them for worldly adventures. She could do this. It would be difficult, but she had the resolve to succeed. She needed to put things right. She needed to help people accept others' ideas and attitudes. She needed to bring peace, tolerance and acceptance to the world. She knew it was a difficult road, but she would succeed.

Tasting the electric charge in the air, Eleanor glanced seawards, towards the horizon. Dark clouds were gathering. *Looks like we're in for a storm*, she thought, when the first of the oversized raindrops fell from the sky. Her observant eye took in every detail, larger than their usual size, falling too slowly, a synthetic material. She wondered about the meaning of it. Eleanor looked over towards Porthenby Island and smiled knowingly, she wasn't troubled… she had been expecting some kind of sign. Turning to study her sister and the musician who were strolling off the beach towards a café hand in hand, she noticed they were oblivious of the weather. It made her feel happy. As she walked home Eleanor began to plan her future; she felt alive.

Enter The Dragons

Chesten held out her hand to catch the first misshaped raindrops. They were wet, wetter than normal and tasted salty. It was peculiar that an unannounced storm could appear from such a sunny start. However, it wasn't unheard of... particularly for Cornish weather. Still, it didn't seem right. She had listened to the weather forecast earlier this morning, and there had been no warning of a storm. No signs of the cows, at Cove Cottage, seeking shelter. No sign of Eleanor and Anna with waterproofs, as they strolled on the beach, and they could read the weather like a book. It was strange.

"Come on, let's go!" someone from the gang shouted. "We'll get drenched out here."

The plump raindrops bounced off the springy grass and drove the teenagers away, far from sight. Freeing the island of unwanted visitors.

"Hurry Ches!" one of her school friends hollered. "The storm's coming!"

"I'm right behind you," she replied, grabbing hold of Tamara and deliberately hanging back from the crowd. She hadn't been able to relax with their friends and was pleased to see them scurrying away from the weather.

She couldn't prevent herself from thinking about the journey into Mermaid Cave, and the treacherous position she had placed her sister and Jack in. How could she have been so stupid? True, they could have said no, but they had been drawn into her adventure when she had made it sound so easy to accomplish. She took full responsibility for all of their actions. Understandably both sets of parents had refused to accept her reasoning and decided they were all equally to blame. She had pleaded her case, but Jack and Tamara refused to let her be their scapegoat. Chesten made a promise to herself that she would never put her sister or Jack, or anyone else, in any dangerous situation again; that was a fact.

"Why aren't we going?" Jack asked, when the last of their friends had abandoned the island.

Soaked to the skin, Chesten replied, "The tide's turning." She led the way onto the bridge, so they could watch the stormy, angry sea churning its way through the strait. The flood tide was eager to regain the ground it had lost earlier in the day. Rain, thunder and lightning tore across the sky, creating a violent backdrop for the forthcoming scene. A privileged, unique, appreciative audience had been selected for the performance.

"Prospero's storm," gasped Tamara.

"Look!" shouted Jack over the howling wind that shook the bridge mercilessly.

And there they were, tumbling and turning as they entered the strait, like two playful puppies. Colourful, energetic, powerful: the twin Dragons. Not yet fully grown but still an impressive size. Playfully crashing into the waves and each other they lacked the grace, confidence and agility of their mother, but that would come… with time.

"What an entrance!" shrieked Chesten.

The twins acknowledged the trio with spectacular leaps and dives in near perfect unison. As they swam under the bridge and turned to enter Mermaid Cave, the sun broke through the clouds.

Pseudonym Katy Booth
Twitter — @KatyBooth45
Facebook — Kay Longden

www.blossomspringpublishing.com

Printed in Great Britain
by Amazon

75715388R00132